William Hope Hodgson was the son of an Essex clergyman. He left home early in life to spend eight years at sea, a period of his life which profoundly influenced his writing career. He voyaged three times round the world and received the Royal Humane Society's medal for saving a life at sea. When World War 1 broke out he was living in the south of France with his wife. He returned to England and was granted a commission in the 171st Brigade of Royal Field Artillery. He fought at Ypres, distinguishing himself for bravery. He was killed in 1918 by a shell whilst on duty.

Hodgson wrote a number of novels, including THE HOUSE ON THE BORDERLAND and THE NIGHT LAND, short stories and poetry and has often been compared with H. P. Lovecraft.

The Boats of the "Glen Carrig"

WILLIAM HOPE HODGSON

SPHERE BOOKS LIMITED
30–32 Gray's Inn Road, London WC1X 8JL

First published in Great Britain by
Sphere Books Ltd 1982
Copyright © 1971 by Lin Carter
Published in the United States of America by
Ballantine Books, Inc. 1971

Printed and bound in Great Britain by
Collins, Glasgow

Contents

About THE BOATS OF THE "GLEN CARRIG,"
and William Hope Hodgson:

STRANGE ODYSSEY

"Now we had been five days in the boats, and in all this time made no discovering of land. Then upon the morning of the sixth day came there a cry from the bo'sun, who had the command of the lifeboat, that there was something which might be land afar upon our larboard bow . . . ."

Thus, without foreword or preamble, *The Boats of the "Glen Carrig"* opens and we are plunged without warning into one of the strangest tales of the sea and its mysteries ever recorded; a novel unique in all literature for its haunting, dreamlike mood of shadowy, spectral strangeness and dim, nightmarish terror. . . .

The history of certain books is a strange odyssey. Books are written and published and fade into obscurity; but they are passed on from hand to hand, from mind to mind, and they find friends who spread the word of them to other congenial spirits—and sometimes a book may lapse into the limbo of the forgotten for years, or decades, or entire generations; but is not quite ever permitted to die.

This is the history of *The Boats of the "Glen Carrig";* and if ever a book had a stranger odyssey I have yet to hear of it.

William Hope Hodgson was born in 1875, the son of an Essex clergyman. He left home as a youth, spent eight years at sea, voyaged thrice around the world, and finally settled in the south of France with his wife just before the outbreak of World War I. At the age of forty he returned to England, was granted a commission in the 171st Brigade of Royal Field Artillery, and fought at Ypres where he distinguished himself for bravery under fire.

In April of 1918 the German army made its great attack. Hodgson and a few other officers and noncommissioned officers stemmed the breakthrough and held their post against an overwhelming number of the enemy; very shortly thereafter he was killed when the Germans shelled an observation post. He was only forty–three. His death cut short a brilliant literary career that was just beginning.

Hodgson's first book, *The Boats of the "Glen Carrig"*, was published in 1907 by the London firm of Chapman and Hall. The first novel of an unknown author of thirty-two, it attracted little notice. During these last eleven years of his short life he published fourteen books; novels, collections of short stories, and two volumes of verse—the last few books published after his death. Although the reviews were good, these were the long, horrible, bloody years of the Great War, and the English-speaking world was in no mood to read haunting tales of nightmare. Also, Hodgson found himself in competition for the attention of those readers who were willing to entertain the macabre against far more famous authors, such as Arthur Machen, M. R. James, and Algernon Blackwood. After Hodgson's death ended a promising career, what little fame he had acquired faded, and his works fell into obscurity.

But *The Boats of the "Glen Carrig"* was too good a book to be forgotten. It was revived thirteen years after its first printing when Holden & Hardingham of London reprinted it in 1920. And eleven years after that, Colin de la Mare included a little-known short story by Hodgson in his Faber & Faber anthology, *They Walk Again*. In America, this book came into the hands of a young fantasy enthusiast named H. C. Koenig . . . and the strange odyssey of *The Boats of the "Glen Carrig"* was truly begun.

Koenig had never heard of Hodgson, or had heard of him but vaguely, and the talent of this unknown British author fascinated him and intrigued his curiosity. He searched for information about Hodgson in standard bibliographical studies of supernatural fiction, but in vain. No one seemed to know of William Hope Hodgson or his work. Koenig searched through scores of anthologies—by Bohun Lynch, Dashiell Hammett, Dorothy Sayers, Montague Summers, T. Everett Harre, Harrison Dale—without finding a single Hodgson tale. Edith Birkhead's pioneering study of the growth of fantastic literature in English, *The Tale of Terror* (1931), contained not a single reference to Hodgson; and even H. P. Lovecraft, in the first version of his excellent monograph, *Supernatural Horror in Literature* (1927), seemed totally unaware of William Hope Hodgson.

But Koenig persevered, eventually interesting British antiquarian bookshops in his search; and they found a few Hodgson first editions for him. Reading Hodgson at length confirmed Koenig's initial impression that here was a neglected master, and he began a campaign to make the small world of fantasy collectors and connoisseurs aware of the stature of this forgotten giant. For years Koenig wrote and talked of Hodgson; tirelessly championed his cause; strove to get Hodgson into print.

A great break-through occurred in 1945, when a condensed version of *The Boats of the "Glen Carrig"* appeared as the lead novel in the June issue of an American magazine called *Famous Fantastic Mysteries*. This magazine printing brought one of Hodgson's major novels to the attention of many thousands of American readers for the first time—and I, at fifteen, was among them. This epochal milestone in the odyssey of *The Boats of the "Glen Carrig"* is entirely due to

H. C. Koenig, who supplied the editrix of the magazine, Mary Gnaedinger, with the text. Miss Gnaedinger also published another novel, *The Ghost Pirates,* and a short tale by Hodgson.

The fiction of William Hope Hodgson was thus brought to the attention of powerful magazines and important critics and collectors. H. P. Lovecraft praised his weird novel *The House on the Borderland* in the highest of terms; Clark Ashton Smith wrote appreciatively of *The Night Land* which many (including myself) consider to be Hodgson's greatest masterpiece, and that greatest American magazine of the macabre and the fantastic, *Weird Tales,* printed at least one of his finest short stories.

A year after *The Boats of the "Glen Carrig"* appeared in *Famous Fantastic Mysteries,* August Derleth, the publisher of Arkham House, was persuaded by Koenig's enthusiasm and brought his campaign to its culmination. In 1946 a mammoth omnibus volume appeared, *The House on the Borderland and Other Novels,* which in 649 closely-printed pages of small type brought into print in this country for the first time the uncut text of Hodgson's four great fantastic novels, with a foreword by H. C. Koenig and a bibliography of Hodgsoniana by A. Langley Searles.

This important book appeared in a limited edition of only three thousand copies and by now has long since gone out of print. But it brought Hodgson the popularity he had long deserved; and thirty years after his death, Hodgson was finally recognized as a great master of supernatural fiction.

The greatness of William Hope Hodgson lies, I would say, in two factors. In the first place, most of the masters of the macabre tale—Bierce, Machen, Poe, Lovecraft, Chambers, Blackwood, Dunsany, James, Le Fanu —worked best in short story length. While they occasionally attempted the novel of supernatural terror, their finest work lay in the short story. *Dracula* towers alone, in my estimation, as virtually the only masterpiece of horror ever written in novel length.

The reason for this preference of the short story over the novel as the medium for superior supernatural fiction is not difficult to understand. The horror tale is primarily one of mood, of suggestive atmosphere; this tenuous mood of terror is very difficult to sustain, and usually is sustained best at short length. Even so mighty a master as Poe could not keep up this mood at novel-length; his *Narrative of Arthur Gordon Pym* is generally considered a failure. But Hodgson, a brilliant artist of the supernatural short story, is every bit as good when working in the novel; and therefore he is almost alone in the field. (*Dracula,* the best example I know of the horror novel, is really abominably written; it succeeds only through the novelty and dramatic power of its conception).

Hodgson's second claim to fame lies in his use of the sea. To my taste, no other writer in history has so wonderfully and perfectly captured the mystery and strangeness, the awe and terror and beauty of that illimitable waste of waters which conceals three quarters of our planet. In this respect, Hodgson comes very close to challenging the supremacy of the great Joseph Conrad; so very close, in fact, that I cannot make up my mind which of the two authors more powerfully suggests the haunting strangeness and wonder of the sea and its mysteries.

It is now a quarter of a century since *The Boats of the "Glen Carrig"* was included in that Arkham House omnibus edition of Hodgson's novels; the book has become rare, a collector's item, and commands high prices. It is time this extraordinary and deeply moving book was brought into print again.

This, the first paperback printing of *The Boats of the "Glen Carrig",* and its first printing in any form since 1946, will bring it to the attention of a whole new generation of readers. The novel is now 64 years old, but its power, simplicity and dreamlike mood have not aged. I doubt if a novel as unique and well-crafted as this will ever again be permitted to lapse into obscurity.

In fact, the strange odyssey of this remarkable book may still be just beginning. . . .

—LIN CARTER
Editorial Consultant:
The Ballantine Adult Fantasy Series

Hollis, Long Island, New York.

The Boats of the "Glen Carrig"

Being an account of their Adventures in the Strange places of the Earth, after the foundering of the good ship Glen Carrig *through striking upon a hidden rock in the unknown seas to the Southward. As told by John Winterstraw, Gent., to his Son James Winterstraw, in the year 1757, and by him committed very properly and legibly to manuscript.*

MADRE MIA

People may say thou art no longer young
    And yet, to me, thy youth was yesterday,
        A yesterday that seems
        Still mingled with my dreams.
Ah! how the years have o'er thee flung
    Their soft mantilla, grey.

And e'en to them thou art not over old;
    How could'st thou be! Thy hair
        Hast scarcely lost its deep old glorious dark:
        Thy face is scarcely lined. No mark
Destroys its calm serenity. Like gold
    Of evening light, when winds scarce stir,
    The soul-light of thy face is pure as prayer.

I: The Land of Lonesomeness

Now we had been five days in the boats, and in all this time made no discovering of land. Then upon the morning of the sixth day came there a cry from the bo'sun, who had the command of the lifeboat, that there was something which might be land afar upon our larboard bow; but it was very low lying, and none could tell whether it was land or but a morning cloud. Yet, because there was the beginning of hope within our breasts, we pulled wearily towards it, and thus, in about an hour, discovered it to be indeed the coast of some flat country.

Then, it might be a little after the hour of midday, we had come so close to it that we could distinguish with ease what manner of land lay beyond the shore, and thus we found it to be of an abominable flatness, desolate beyond all that I could have imagined. Here and there it appeared to be covered with clumps of queer vegetation; though whether they were small trees or great bushes, I had no means of telling; but this I know, that they were like unto nothing which ever I had set eyes upon before.

So much as this I gathered as we pulled slowly along the coast, seeking an opening whereby we could pass inward to the land; but a weary time passed or ere

1

we came upon that which we sought. Yet, in the end, we found it—a slimy-banked creek, which proved to be the estuary of a great river, though we spoke of it always as a creek. Into this we entered, and proceeded at no great pace upwards along its winding course; and as we made forward, we scanned the low banks upon each side, perchance there might be some spot where we could make to land; but we found none—the banks being composed of a vile mud which gave us no encouragement to venture rashly upon them.

Now, having taken the boat something over a mile up the great creek, we came upon the first of that vegetation which I had chanced to notice from the sea, and here, being within some score yards of it, we were the better able to study it. Thus I found that it was indeed composed largely of a sort of tree, very low and stunted, and having what might be described as an unwholesome look about it. The branches of this tree, I perceived to be the cause of my inability to recognize it from a bush, until I had come close upon it; for they grew thin and smooth through all their length, and hung towards the earth; being weighted thereto by a single, large cabbage-like plant which seemed to sprout from the extreme tip of each.

Presently, having passed beyond this first clump of the vegetation, and the banks of the river remaining very low, I stood me upon a thwart, by which means I was enabled to scan the surrounding country. This I discovered, so far as my sight could penetrate, to be pierced in all directions with innumerable creeks and pools, some of these latter being very great of extent; and, as I have before made mention, everywhere the country was low set—as it might be a great plain of mud; so that it gave me a sense of dreariness to look out upon it. It may be, all unconsciously, that my spirit was put in awe by the extreme silence of all the country around; for in all that waste I could see no living thing, neither bird nor vegetable, save it be the stunted trees, which, indeed, grew in clumps here and there over all the land, so much as I could see.

This silence, when I grew fully aware of it was the more uncanny; for my memory told me that never before had I come upon a country which contained so much quietness. Nothing moved across my vision—not even a lone bird soared up against the dull sky; and, for my hearing, not so much as the cry of a sea-bird came to me—no! nor the croak of a frog, nor the plash of a fish. It was as though we had come upon the Country of Silence, which some have called the Land of Lonesomeness.

Now three hours had passed whilst we ceased not to labour at the oars, and we could no more see the sea; yet no place fit to our feet had come to view, for everywhere the mud, grey and black, surrounded us—encompassing us veritably by a slimy wilderness. And so we were fain to pull on, in the hope that we might come ultimately to firm ground.

Then, a little before sundown, we halted upon our oars, and made a scant meal from a portion of our remaining provisions; and as we ate, I could see the sun sinking away over the wastes, and I had some slight diversion in watching the grotesque shadows which it cast from the trees into the water upon our larboard side; for we had come to a pause opposite a clump of the vegetation. It was at this time, as I remember, that it was borne in upon me afresh how very silent was the land; and that this was not due to my imagination, I remarked that the men both in our own and in the bo'sun's boat, seemed uneasy because of it; for none spoke save in undertones, as though they had fear of breaking it.

And it was at this time, when I was awed by so much solitude, that there came the first telling of life in all that wilderness. I heard it first in the far distance, away inland—a curious, low, sobbing note it was, and the rise and the fall of it was like to the sobbing of a lonesome wind through a great forest. Yet was there no wind. Then, in a moment, it had died, and the silence of the land was awesome by reason of the contrast. And I looked about me at the men, both in the boat in which I was and that which the bo'sun commanded; and not one was there but held himself in a posture of listening. In this wise a minute of quietness passed, and then one of the men gave out a laugh, born of the nervousness which had taken him.

The bo'sun muttered to him to hush, and, in the same moment, there came again the plaint of that wild sobbing. And abruptly it sounded away on our right, and immediately was caught up, as it were, and echoed back from some place beyond us afar up the creek. At that, I got me upon a thwart, intending to take another look over the country about us; but the banks of the creek had become higher; moreover the vegetation acted as a screen, even had my stature and elevation enabled me to overlook the banks.

And so, after a little while, the crying died away, and there was another silence. Then, as we sat each one harking for what might next befall, George, the youngest 'prentice boy, who had his seat beside me, plucked me by the sleeve, inquiring in a troubled voice whether I had any knowledge of that which the crying might portend; but I shook my head, telling him that I had no knowing beyond his own; though, for his comfort, I said that it might be the wind. Yet, at that, he shook his head; for indeed, it was plain that it could not be by such agency for there was a stark calm.

Now, I had scarce made an end of my remark, when again the sad crying was upon us. It appeared to come from far up the creek, and from far down the creek, and from inland and the land between us and the sea. It filled the evening air with its doleful wailing, and I remarked that there was in it a curious sobbing, most human in its despairful crying. And so awesome was the thing that no man of us spoke; for it seemed that we harked to the weeping of lost souls. And then, as we waited fearfully, the sun sank below the edge of the world, and the dusk was upon us.

, And now a more extraordinary thing happened; for, as the night fell with swift gloom, the strange wailing and crying was hushed, and another sound stole out upon the land—a far, sullen growling. At the first, like the crying, it came from far inland; but was caught up speedily on all sides of us, and presently the dark was full of it. And it increased in volume, and strange trumpetings fled across it. Then, though with slowness, it fell away to a low, continuous growling, and in it there was that which I can only describe as an insistent, hungry snarl. Aye! no other word of which I have knowledge so well describes it as that—a note of *hunger,* most awesome to the ear. And this, more than all the rest of those incredible voicings, brought terror into my heart.

Now as I sat listening, George gripped me suddenly by the arm, declaring in a shrill whisper that something had come among the clump of trees upon the left-hand bank. Of the truth of this, I had immediately a proof; for I caught the sound of a continuous rustling among them, and then a nearer note of growling, as though a wild beast purred at my elbow. Immediately upon this, I caught the bo'sun's voice, calling in a low tone to Josh, the eldest 'prentice, who had the charge of our boat, to come alongside of him; for he would have the boats together. Then got we out the oars and laid the boats together in the midst of the creek; and so we watched through the night, being full of fear, so that we kept our speech low; that is, so low as would carry our thoughts one to the other through the noise of the growling.

And so the hours passed, and naught happened more than I have told, save that once, a little after midnight, the trees opposite to us seemed to be stirred again, as though some creature, or creatures, lurked among them; and there came, a little after that, a sound as of something stirring the water up against the bank; but it ceased in a while and the silence fell once more.

Thus, after a weariful time, away Eastwards the sky began to tell of the coming of the day; and, as the light grew and strengthened, so did that insatiable growling pass hence with the dark and the shadows. And so at last came the day, and once more there was borne to us the sad wailing that had preceded the night. For a certain while it lasted, rising and falling most mournfully over the vastness of the surrounding wastes, until the sun was risen some degrees above the horizon; after which it began to fail, dying away in lingering echoes, most solemn to our ears. And so it passed, and there came again the silence that had been with us in all the daylight hours.

Now, it being day, the bo'sun bade us make such sparse breakfast as our provender allowed; after which, having first scanned the banks to discern if any fearful thing were visible, we took again to our oars, and proceeded on our upward journey; for we hoped presently to come upon a country where life had not become extinct, and where we could put foot to honest earth. Yet, as I have made mention earlier, the vegetation, where it grew, did flourish most luxuriantly; so that I am scarce correct when I speak of life as being extinct in that land. For, indeed, now I think of it, I can remember that the very mud from which it sprang seemed veritably to have a fat, sluggish life of its own, so rich and viscid was it.

Presently it was midday; yet was there but little change in the nature of the surrounding wastes; though it may be that the vegetation was something thicker, and more continuous along the banks. But the banks were still of the same thick, clinging mud; so that nowhere could we effect a landing; though, had we, the rest of the country beyond the banks seemed no better.

And all the while, as we pulled, we glanced continuously from bank to bank; and those who worked not at the oars were fain to rest a hand by their sheath-knives; for the happenings of the past night were continually in our minds, and we were in great fear; so that we had turned back to the sea but that we had come so nigh to the end of our provisions.

II: The Ship in the Creek

THEN, IT WAS NIGH ON TO EVENING, WE CAME UPON a creek opening into the greater one through the bank upon our left. We had been like to pass it—as, indeed, we had passed many throughout the day—but that the bo'sun, whose boat had the lead, cried out that there was some craft lying-up, a little beyond the first bend. And, indeed, so it seemed; for one of the masts of her —all jagged, where it had carried away—stuck up plain to our view.

Now, having grown sick with so much lonesomeness, and being in fear of the approaching night, we gave out something near to a cheer, which, however, the bo'sun silenced, having no knowledge of those who might occupy the stranger. And so, in silence, the bo'sun turned his craft toward the creek, whereat we followed, taking heed to keep quietness, and working the oars warily. So, in a little, we came to the shoulder of the bend, and had plain sight of the vessel some little way beyond us. From the distance she had no appearance of being inhabited; so that after some small hesitation, we pulled towards her, though still being at pains to keep silence.

The strange vessel lay against that bank of the creek which was upon our right, and over above her was a thick clump of the stunted trees. For the rest, she appeared to be firmly imbedded in the heavy mud, and there was a certain look of age about her which carried to me a doleful suggestion that we should find naught aboard of her fit for an honest stomach.

We had come to a distance of maybe some ten fathoms from her starboard bow—for she lay with her head down towards the mouth of the little creek—when the bo'sun bade his men to back water, the which Josh did regarding our own boat. Then, being ready to fly if we had been in danger, the bo'sun hailed the stranger; but got no reply, save that some echo of his shout seemed to come back at us. And so he sung out again to her, chance there might be some below decks who had not caught his first hail; but, for the second time, no answer came to us, save the low echo—naught, but that the silent trees took on a little quivering, as though his voice had shaken them.

At that, being confident now within our minds, we laid alongside, and, in a minute had shinned up the oars and so gained her decks. Here, save that the glass of the skylight of the main cabin had been broken, and some portion of the framework shattered, there was no extraordinary litter; so that it appeared to us as though she had been no great while abandoned.

So soon as the bo'sun had made his way up from the boat, he turned aft toward the scuttle, the rest of us following. We found the leaf of the scuttle pulled forward to within an inch of closing, and so much effort did it require of us to push it back, that we had immediate evidence of a considerable time since any had gone down that way.

However, it was no great while before we were below, and here we found the main cabin to be empty, save for the bare furnishings. From it there opened off two staterooms at the forrard end, and the captain's cabin in the after part, and in all of these we found matters of clothing and sundries such as proved that the vessel had been deserted apparently in haste. In further proof of this we found, in a drawer in the captain's room, a considerable quantity of loose gold, the which it was not to be supposed would have been left by the free-will of the owner.

Of the state-rooms, the one upon the starboard side gave evidence that it had been occupied by a woman—no doubt a passenger. The other, in which there were two bunks, had been shared, so far as we could have any certainty, by a couple of young men; and this we gathered by observation of various garments which were scattered carelessly about.

Yet it must not be supposed that we spent any great time in the cabins; for we were pressed for food, and made haste—under the directing of the bo'sun—to discover if the hulk held victuals whereby we might be kept alive.

To this end, we removed the hatch which led down to the lazarette, and, lighting two lamps which we had with us in the boats, went down to make a search. And so, in a little while, we came upon two casks which the bo'sun broke open with a hatchet. These casks were sound and tight, and in them was ship's biscuit, very good and fit for food. At this, as may be imagined, we felt eased in our minds, knowing that there was no immediate fear of starvation. Following this, we found a barrel of molasses; a cask of rum; some cases of dried fruit—these were mouldy and scarce fit to be eaten; a cask of salt beef, another of pork; a small barrel of vinegar; a case of brandy; two barrels of flour—one of which proved to be damp-struck; and a bunch of tallow dips.

In a little while we had all these things up in the big cabin, so that we might come at them the better to make choice of that which was fit for our stomachs, and that which was otherwise. Meantime, whilst the bo'sun over-hauled these matters, Josh called a couple of the men, and went on deck to bring up the gear from the boats, for it had been decided that we should pass the night aboard the hulk.

When this was accomplished, Josh took a walk forrard to the fo'cas'le; but found nothing beyond two seamen's chests; a sea-bag, and some odd gear. There were, indeed, no more than ten bunks in the place; for she was but a small brig, and had no call for a great crowd. Yet Josh was more than a little puzzled to know what had come to the odd chests; for it was not to be supposed that there had been no more than two—and a sea-bag—among ten men. But to this, at that time, he had no answer, and so, being sharp for supper, made a return to the deck, and thence to the main cabin.

Now while he had been gone, the bo'sun had set the men to clearing out the main cabin; after which, he had served out two biscuits apiece all round, and a tot of rum. To Josh, when he appeared, he gave the same, and, in a little, we called a sort of council; being sufficiently stayed by the food to talk.

Yet, before we came to speech, we made shift to light our pipes; for the bo'sun had discovered a case of tobacco in the captain's cabin, and after this we came to the consideration of our position.

We had provender, so the bo'sun calculated, to last us for the better part of two months, and this without any great stint; but we had yet to prove if the brig held water in her casks, for that in the creek was brackish, even so far as we had penetrated from the sea; else we had not been in need. To the charge of this, the bo'sun set Josh, along with two of the men. Another, he told to take charge of the galley, so long as we were in the hulk. But for that night, he said we had no need to do aught; for we had sufficient of water in the boats' breakers to last us till the morrow. And so, in a little, the dusk began to fill the cabin; but we talked on, being greatly content with our present ease and the good tobacco which we enjoyed.

In a little while, one of the men cried out suddenly to us to be silent, and, in that minute, all heard it—a far, drawn-out wailing; the same which had come to us in the evening of the first day. At that we looked at one another through the smoke and the growing dark, and, even as we looked, it became plainer heard, until, in a while, it was all about us—aye! it seemed to come floating down through the broken framework of the skylight as though some weariful, unseen thing stood and cried upon the decks above our heads.

Now through all that crying, none moved; none, that is, save Josh and the bo'sun, and they went up into the scuttle to see whether anything was in sight; but they found nothing, and so came down to us; for there was no wisdom in exposing ourselves, unarmed as we were, save for our sheath-knives.

And so, in a little, the night crept down upon the world, and still we sat within the dark cabin, none speaking, and knowing of the rest only by the glows of their pipes.

All at once there came a low, muttered growl, stealing across the land; and immediately the crying was quenched in its sullen thunder. It died away, and there was a full minute of silence; then, once more it came, and it was nearer and more plain to the ear. I took my pipe from my mouth; for I had come again upon the great fear and uneasiness which the happenings of the first night had bred in me, and the taste of the smoke brought me no more pleasure. The muttered growl swept over our heads and died away into the distance, and there was a sudden silence.

Then, in that quietness, came the bo'sun's voice. He was bidding us haste every one into the captain's cabin. As we moved to obey him, he ran to draw over the lid of the scuttle; and Josh went with him, and, together, they had it across; though with difficulty. When we had come into the captain's cabin, we closed and barred the door, piling two great sea-chests up against it; and so we felt near safe; for we knew that no thing, man nor beast, could come at us there. Yet, as may be supposed, we felt not altogether secure; for there was that in the growling which now filled the darkness, that seemed demoniac, and we knew not what horrid Powers were abroad.

And so through the night the growling continued, seeming to be mighty near unto us—aye! almost over our heads, and of a loudness far surpassing all that had come to us on the previous night; so that I thanked the Almighty that we had come into shelter in the midst of so much fear.

III: The Thing That Made Search

NOW AT TIMES, I FELL UPON SLEEP, AS DID MOST OF
the others; but, for the most part, I lay half sleeping and
half waking—being unable to attain to true sleep by
reason of the everlasting growling above us in the night,
and the fear which it bred in me. Thus, it chanced that
just after midnight, I caught a sound in the main cabin
beyond the door, and immediately I was fully waked. I
sat me up and listened, and so became aware that
something was fumbling about the deck of the main
cabin. At that, I got to my feet and made my way to
where the bo'sun lay, meaning to waken him, if he
slept; but he caught me by the ankle, as I stooped to
shake him, and whispered to me to keep silence; for he
too had been aware of that strange noise of something
fumbling beyond in the big cabin.

In a little, we crept both of us so close to the door as
the chests would allow, and there we crouched, listening; but could not tell what manner of thing it might be
which produced so strange a noise. For it was neither
shuffling, nor treading of any kind, nor yet was it the
whirr of a bat's wings, the which had first occurred to
me, knowing how vampires are said to inhabit the
nights in dismal places. Nor yet was it the slurr of a

snake; but rather it seemed to us to be as though a great wet cloth were being rubbed everywhere across the floor and bulkheads. We were the better able to be certain of the truth of this likeness, when, suddenly, it passed across the further side of the door behind which we listened: at which, you may be sure, we drew backwards both of us in fright; though the door, and the chests, stood between us and that which rubbed against it.

Presently, the sound ceased, and, listen as we might, we could no longer distinguish it. Yet, until the morning, we dozed no more; being troubled in mind as to what manner of thing it was which had made search in the big cabin.

Then in time the day came, and the growling ceased. For a mournful while the sad crying filled our ears, and then at last the eternal silence that fills the day hours of that dismal land fell upon us.

So, being at last in quietness, we slept, being greatly awearied. About seven in the morning, the bo'sun waked me, and I found that they had opened the door into the big cabin; but though the bo'sun and I made careful search, we could nowhere come upon anything to tell us aught concerning the thing which had put us so in fright. Yet, I know not if I am right in saying that we came upon nothing; for, in several places, the bulkheads had a *chafed* look; but whether this had been there before that night, we had no means of telling.

Of that which we had heard, the bo'sun bade me make no mention, for he would not have the men put more in fear than need be. This I conceived to be wisdom, and so held my peace. Yet I was much troubled in my mind to know what manner of thing it was which we had need to fear, and more—I desired greatly to know whether we should be free of it in the daylight hours; for there was always with me, as I went hither and thither, the thought that IT—for that is how

I designated it in my mind—might come upon us to our destruction.

Now after breakfast, at which we had each a portion of salt pork, besides rum and biscuit (for by now the fire in the caboose had been set going), we turned-to at various matters, under the directing of the bo'sun. Josh and two of the men made examination of the water casks, and the rest of us lifted the main hatch-covers, to make inspection of her cargo; but lo! we found nothing, save some three feet of water in her hold.

By this time, Josh had drawn some water off from the casks; but it was most unsuitable for drinking, being vile of smell and taste. Yet the bo'sun bade him draw some into buckets, so that the air might haply purify it; but though this was done, and the water allowed to stand through the morning, it was but little better.

At this, as might be imagined, we were exercised in our minds as to the manner in which we should come upon suitable water; for by now we were beginning to be in need of it. Yet though one said one thing, and another said another, no one had wit enough to call to mind any method by which our need should be satisfied. Then, when we had made an end of dining, the bo'sun sent Josh, with four of the men, up stream, perchance after a mile or two the water should prove of sufficient freshness to meet our purpose. Yet they returned a little before sundown having no water; for everywhere it was salt.

Now the bo'sun, foreseeing that it might be impossible to come upon water, had set the man whom he had ordained to be our cook, to boiling the creek water in three great kettles. This he had ordered to be done soon after the boat left; and over the spout of each, he had hung a great pot of iron, filled with cold water from the hold—this being cooler than that from the creek—so that the steam from each kettle impinged upon the cold surface of the iron pots, and being by this means condensed, was caught in three buckets placed beneath them upon the floor of the caboose. In this way, enough water was collected to supply us for the evening and the following morning; yet it was but a slow method, and we had sore need of a speedier, were we to leave the hulk so soon as I, for one, desired.

We made our supper before sunset, so as to be free of the crying which we had reason to expect. After that, the bo'sun shut the scuttle, and we went every one of us into the captain's cabin, after which we barred the door, as on the previous night; and well was it for us that we acted with this prudence.

By the time that we had come into the captain's cabin, and secured the door, it was upon sunsetting, and as the dusk came on, so did the melancholy wailing pass over the land; yet, being by now somewhat inured to so much strangeness, we lit our pipes, and smoked; though I observed that none talked; for the crying without was not to be forgotten.

Now, as I have said, we kept silence; but this was only for a time, and our reason for breaking it was a discovery made by George, the younger apprentice. This lad, being no smoker, was fain to do something to while away the time, and with this intent, he had raked out the contents of a small box, which had lain upon the deck at the side of the forrard bulkhead.

The box had appeared filled with odd small lumber of which a part was a dozen or so grey paper wrappers, such as are used, I believe, for carrying samples of corn; though I have seen them put to other purposes, as, indeed, was now the case. At first George had tossed these aside; but it growing darker the bo'sun lit one of the candles which we had found in the lazarette. Thus, George, who was proceeding to tidy back the rubbish which was cumbering the place, discovered something which caused him to cry out to us his astonishment.

Now, upon hearing George call out, the bo'sun bade him keep silence, thinking it was but a piece of boyish restlessness; but George drew the candle to him, and bade us to listen; for the wrappers were covered with fine handwriting after the fashion of a woman's.

Even as George told us of that which he had found we became aware that the night was upon us; for suddenly the crying ceased, and in place thereof there came out of the far distance the low thunder of the night-growling, that had tormented us through the past two nights. For a space, we ceased to smoke, and sat—listening; for it was a very fearsome sound. In a very little while it seemed to surround the ship, as on the previous nights; but at length, using ourselves to it, we resumed our smoking, and bade George to read out to us from the writing upon the paper wrappers.

Then George, though shaking somewhat in his voice, began to decipher that which was upon the wrappers, and a strange and awesome story it was, and bearing much upon our own concerns:—

"Now, when they discovered the spring among the trees that crown the bank, there was much rejoicing; for we had come to have much need of water. And some, being in fear of the ship (declaring, because of all our misfortune and the strange disappearances of their messmates and the brother of my lover, that she was haunted by a devil), declared their intention of taking their gear up to the spring, and there making a camp. This they conceived and carried out in the space of one afternoon; though our Captain, a good and true man, begged of them, as they valued life, to stay within the shelter of their living-place. Yet, as I have remarked, they would none of them hark to his counselling, and, because the Mate and the bo'sun were gone he had no means of compelling them to wisdom—"

At this point, George ceased to read, and began to

rustle among the wrappers, as though in search for the continuation of the story.

Presently he cried out that he could not find it, and dismay was upon his face.

But the bo'sun told him to read on from such sheets as were left; for, as he observed, we had no knowledge if more existed; and we were fain to know further of that spring, which, from the story, appeared to be over the bank near to the vessel.

George, being thus adjured, picked up the topmost sheet; for they were, as I heard him explain to the bo'sun, all oddly numbered, and having but little reference one to the other. Yet we were mightily keen to know even so much as such odd scraps might tell unto us. Whereupon, George read from the next wrapper, which ran thus:—

"Now, suddenly, I heard the Captain cry out that there was something in the main cabin, and immediately my lover's voice calling to me to lock my door, and on no condition to open it. Then the door of the Captain's cabin slammed, and there came a silence, and the silence was broken by a *sound*. Now, this was the first time that I had heard the Thing make search through the big cabin; but, afterwards, my lover told me it had happened aforetime, and they had told me naught, fearing to frighten me needlessly; though now I understood why my lover had bidden me never to leave my stateroom door unbolted in the nighttime. I remember also, wondering if the noise of breaking glass that had waked me somewhat from my dreams a night or two previously, had been the work of this indescribable Thing; for on the morning following that night, the glass in the skylight had been smashed. Thus it was that my thoughts wandered out to trifles, while yet my soul seemed ready to leap out from my bosom with fright.

"I had, by reason of usage, come to ability to sleep despite of the fearsome growling; for I had conceived its cause to be the mutter of spirits in the night, and had not allowed myself to be unnecessarily frightened with doleful thoughts; for my lover had assured me of our safety, and that we should yet come to our home. And now, beyond my door, I could hear that fearsome sound of the Thing searching—"

George came to a sudden pause; for the bo'sun had risen and put a great hand upon his shoulder. The lad made to speak; but the bo'sun beckoned to him to say no word, and at that we, who had grown to nervousness through the happenings in the story, began every one to listen. Thus we heard a sound which had escaped us in the noise of the growling without the vessel, and the interest of the reading.

For a space we kept very silent, no man doing more than let the breath go in and out of his body, and so each one of us knew that something moved without, in the big cabin. In a little, something touched upon our door, and it was, as I have mentioned earlier, as though a great swab rubbed and scrubbed at the woodwork. At this, the men nearest unto the door came backwards in a surge, being put in sudden fear by reason of the Thing being so near; but the bo'sun held up a hand, bidding them, in a low voice, to make no unneedful noise. Yet, as though the sounds of their moving had been heard, the door was shaken with such violence that we waited, everyone, expecting to see it torn from its hinges; but it stood, and we hasted to brace it by means of the bunk boards, which we placed between it and the two great chests, and upon these we set a third chest, so that the door was quite hid.

Now, I have no remembrance whether I have put down that when we came first to the ship, we had found the stern window upon the larboard side to be shattered; but so it was, and the bo'sun had closed it by means of a teak-wood cover which was made to go over it in stormy weather, with stout battens across, which were set tight with wedges. This he had done upon the first night, having fear that some evil thing might come upon us through the opening, and very prudent was this same action of his, as shall be seen. Then George cried out that something was at the cover of the larboard window, and we stood back, growing ever more fearful because that some evil creature was so eager to come at us. But the bo'sun, who was a very courageous man, and calm withal, walked over to the closed window, and saw to it that the battens were secure; for he had knowledge sufficient to be sure, if this were so, that no creature with strength less than that of a whale could break it down, and in such case its bulk would assure us from being molested.

Then, even as he made sure of the fastenings, there came a cry of fear from some of the men; for there had come at the glass of the unbroken window, a reddish mass, which plunged up against it, sucking upon it, as it were. Then Josh, who was nearest to the table, caught up the candle, and held it towards the Thing; thus I saw that it had the appearance of a many-flapped thing shaped as it might be, out of raw beef—*but it was alive*.

At this, we stared, everyone being too bemused with terror to do aught to protect ourselves, even had we been possessed of weapons. And as we remained thus, an instant, like silly sheep awaiting the butcher, I heard the framework creak and crack, and there ran splits all across the glass. In another moment, the whole thing would have been torn away, and the cabin undefended, but that the bo'sun, with a great curse at us for our land-lubberly lack of use, seized the other cover, and clapped it over the window. At that, there was more help than could be made to avail, and the battens and wedges were in place in a trice. That this was no sooner accomplished than need be, we had immediate proof; for there came a rending of wood and a splintering of glass, and after that a strange yowling out in the dark, and the yowling rose above and drowned the continuous growling that filled the night. In a little, it died away, and in the brief silence that seemed to ensue, we heard a slobby fumbling at the teak cover; but it was well secured, and we had no immediate cause for fear.

IV: The Two Faces

OF THE REMAINDER OF THAT NIGHT, I HAVE BUT A confused memory. At times we heard the door shaken behind the great chests; but no harm came to it. And, odd whiles, there was a soft thudding and rubbing upon the decks over our heads, and once, as I recollect, the Thing made a final try at the teak covers across the windows; but the day came at last, and found me sleeping. Indeed, we had slept beyond the noon, but that the bo'sun, mindful of our needs, waked us, and we removed the chests. Yet, for perhaps the space of a minute, none durst open the door, until the bo'sun bid us stand to one side. We faced about at him then, and saw that he held a great cutlass in his right hand.

He called to us that there were four more of the weapons, and made a backward motion with his left hand towards an open locker. At that, as might be supposed, we made some haste to the place to which he pointed, and found that, among some other gear, there were three more weapons such as he held; but the fourth was a straight cut-and-thrust, and this I had the good fortune to secure.

Being now armed, we ran to join the bo'sun; for by this he had the door open, and was scanning the main cabin. I would remark here how a good weapon doth seem to put heart into a man; for I, who but a few, short hours since had feared for my life, was now right full of lustiness and fight; which, mayhap, was no matter for regret.

From the main cabin, the bo'sun led up on to the deck, and I remember some surprise at finding the lid of the scuttle even as we had left it the previous night; but then I recollected that the skylight was broken, and there was access to the big cabin that way. Yet, I questioned within myself as to what manner of thing it could be which ignored the convenience of the scuttle, and descended by way of the broken skylight.

We made a search of the decks and fo'cas'le, but found nothing, and, after that, the bo'sun stationed two of us on guard, whilst the rest went about such duties as were needful. In a little, we came to breakfast, and, after that, we prepared to test the story upon the sample wrappers and see perchance whether there was indeed a spring of fresh water among the trees.

Now between the vessel and the trees, lay a slope of the thick mud, against which the vessel rested. To have scrambled up this bank had been next to impossible, by reason of its fat richness; for, indeed, it looked fit to crawl; but that Josh called out to the bo'sun that he had come upon a ladder, lashed across the fo'cas'le head. This was brought, also several hatch covers. The latter were placed first upon the mud, and the ladder laid upon them; by which means we were enabled to pass up to the top of the bank without contact with the mud.

Here, we entered at once among the trees; for they grew right up to the edge; but we had no trouble in making a way; for they were nowhere close together; but standing, rather, each one in a little open space by itself.

We had gone a little way among the trees, when, suddenly, one who was with us cried out that he could see something away on our right, and we clutched everyone his weapon the more determinedly, and went towards it. Yet it proved to be but a seaman's chest, and a space further off, we discovered another. And so, after a little walking, we found the camp; but there was small semblance of a camp about it; for the sail of which the tent had been formed, was all torn and stained, and lay muddy upon the ground. Yet the spring was all we had wished, clear and sweet, and so we knew we might dream of deliverance.

Now, upon our discovery of the spring, it might be thought that we should set up a shout to those upon the vessel; but this was not so; for there was something in the air of the place which cast a gloom upon our spirits, and we had no disinclination to return unto the vessel.

Upon coming to the brig, the bo'sun called to four of the men to go down into the boats, and pass up the breakers: also, he collected all the buckets belonging to the brig, and forthwith each of us was set to our work. Some, those with the weapons, entered into the wood, and gave down the water to those stationed upon the bank, and these, in turn, passed it to those in the vessel. To the man in the galley, the bo'sun gave command to fill a boiler with some of the most select pieces of the pork and beef from the casks and get them cooked so soon as might be, and so we were kept at it; for it had been determined—now that we had come upon water —that we should stay not an hour longer in that monster-ridden craft, and we were all agog to get the boats revictualled, and put back to the sea, from which we had too gladly escaped.

So we worked through all that remainder of the morning, and right on into the afternoon; for we were in mortal fear of the coming dark. Towards four o'clock, the bo'sun sent the man, who had been set to do our cooking, up to us with slices of salt meat upon biscuits, and we ate as we worked, washing our throats with water from the spring, and so, before the evening, we had filled our breakers, and near every vessel which was convenient for us to take in the boats. More, some of us snatched the chance to wash our bodies; for we were sore with brine, having dipped in the sea to keep down thirst as much as might be.

Now, though it had not taken us so great a while to make a finish of our water-carrying if matters had been more convenient; yet because of the softness of the ground under our feet, and the care with which we had to pick our steps, and some little distance between us and the brig, it had grown later than we desired, before we had made an end. Therefore, when the bo'sun sent word that we should come aboard, and bring our gear, we made all haste. Thus, as it chanced, I found that I had left my sword beside the spring, having placed it there to have two hands for the carrying of one of the breakers. At my remarking my loss, George, who stood near, cried out that he would run for it, and was gone in a moment, being greatly curious to see the spring.

Now, at this moment, the bo'sun came up, and called for George; but I informed him that he had run to the spring to bring me my sword. At this, the bo'sun stamped his foot, and swore a great oath, declaring that he had kept the lad by him all the day; having a wish to keep him from any danger which the wood might hold, and knowing the lad's desire to adventure there. At this, a matter which I should have known, I reproached myself for so gross a piece of stupidity, and hastened after the bo'sun, who had disappeared over the top of the bank. I saw his back as he passed into the wood, and ran until I was up with him; for, suddenly, as it were, I found that a sense of chilly dampness had come among the trees; though a while before the place had been full of the warmth of the sun. This, I put to the account of evening, which was drawing on apace; and also, it must be borne in mind, that there were but the two of us.

We came to the spring; but George was not to be

seen, and I saw no sign of my sword. At this, the bo'sun raised his voice, and cried out the lad's name. Once he called, and again; then at the second shout we heard the boy's shrill halloo, from some distance ahead among the trees. At that, we ran towards the sound, plunging heavily across the ground, which was everywhere covered with a thick scum, that clogged the feet in walking. As we ran, we hallooed, and so came upon the boy, and I saw that he had my sword.

The bo'sun ran towards him, and caught him by the arm, speaking with anger, and commanding him to return with us immediately to the vessel.

But the lad, for reply, pointed with my sword, and we saw that he pointed at what appeared to be a bird against the trunk of one of the trees. This, as I moved closer, I perceived to be a part of the tree, and no bird; but it had a very wondrous likeness to a bird; so much so that I went up to it, to see if my eyes had deceived me. Yet it seemed no more than a freak of nature, though most wondrous in its fidelity; being but an excrescence upon the trunk. With a sudden thought that it would make me a curio, I reached up to see whether I could break it away from the tree; but it was above my reach, so that I had to leave it. Yet, one thing I discovered; for, in stretching towards the protuberance, I had placed a hand upon the tree, and its trunk was soft as pulp under my fingers, much after the fashion of a mushroom.

As we turned to go, the bo'sun inquired of George his reason for going beyond the spring, and George told him that he had seemed to hear someone calling to him among the trees, and there had been so much pain in the voice that he had run towards it; but been unable to discover the owner. Immediately afterwards he had seen the curious, bird-like excrescence upon a tree nearby. Then we had called, and of the rest we had knowledge.

We had come nigh to the spring on our return journey, when a sudden low whine seemed to run among the trees. I glanced towards the sky, and realized that the evening was upon us. I was about to remark upon this to the bo'sun, when, abruptly, he came to a stand, and bent forward to stare into the shadows to our right. At that, George and I turned ourselves about to perceive what matter it was which had attracted the attention of the bo'sun; thus we made out a tree some twenty yards away, which had all its branches wrapped about its trunk, much as the lash of a whip is wound about its stock. Now this seemed to us a very strange sight, and we made all of us toward it, to learn the reason of so extraordinary a happening.

Yet, when we had come close upon it, we had no means of arriving at a knowledge of that which it portended; but walked each of us around the tree, and were more astonished, after our circumnavigation of the great vegetable than before.

Now, suddenly, and in the distance, I caught the far wailing that came before the night, and abruptly, as it seemed to me, the tree wailed at us. At that I was vastly astonished and frightened; yet, though I retreated, I could not withdraw my gaze from the tree; but scanned it the more intently; and, suddenly, I saw a brown, human face peering at us from between the wrapped branches. At this, I stood very still, being seized with that fear which renders one shortly incapable of movement. Then, before I had possession of myself, I saw that it was of a part with the trunk of the tree; for I could not tell where it ended and the tree began.

Then I caught the bo'sun by the arm, and pointed; for whether it was a part of the tree or not, it was a work of the devil; but the bo'sun, on seeing it, ran straightway so close to the tree that he might have touched it with his hand, and I found myself beside him. Now, George, who was on the bo'sun's other side, whispered that there was another face, not unlike to a woman's, and, indeed, so soon as I perceived it, I saw that the tree had a second excrescence, most strangely after the face of a woman. Then the bo'sun cried out with an oath, at the strangeness of the thing, and I felt the arm, which I held, shake somewhat, as it might be with a deep emotion. Then, far away, I heard again the sound of the wailing and, immediately, from among the trees about us, there came answering wails and a great sighing. And before I had time to be more than aware of these things, the tree wailed again at us. And at that, the bo'sun cried out suddenly that he knew; though of what it was that he *knew,* I had at that time no knowledge. And, immediately, he began with his cutlass to strike at the tree before us, and to cry upon God to blast it; and lo! at his smiting a very fearsome thing happened; for the tree did bleed like any live creature. Thereafter, a great yowling came from it, and it began to writhe. And, suddenly, I became aware that all about us the trees were a-quiver.

Then George cried out, and ran round upon my side of the bo'sun, and I saw that one of the great cabbage-like things pursued him upon its stem, even as an evil serpent; and very dreadful it was, for it had become blood red in color; but I smote it with the sword, which I had taken from the lad, and it fell to the ground.

Now from the brig I heard them hallooing, and the trees had become like live things, and there was a vast growling in the air, and hideous trumpetings. Then I caught the bo'sun again by the arm, and shouted to him that we must run for our lives; and this we did, smiting with our swords as we ran; for there came things at us, out from the growing dusk.

Thus we made the brig, and, the boats being ready, I scrambled after the bo'sun into his, and we put straight-way into the creek, all of us, pulling with so much haste as our loads would allow. As we went I looked back at the brig, and it seemed to me that a multitude of things hung over the bank above her, and there seemed a flicker of things moving hither and thither aboard of her. And then we were in the great creek up which we had come, and so, in a little, it was night.

All that night we rowed, keeping very strictly to the center of the big creek, and all about us bellowed the vast growling, being more fearsome than ever I had heard it, until it seemed to me that we had waked all that land of terror to a knowledge of our presence. But, when the morning came, so good a speed had we made, what with our fear, and the current being with us, that we were nigh upon the open sea; whereat each one of us raised a shout, feeling like freed prisoners.

And so, full of thankfulness to the Almighty, we rowed outward to the sea.

V: The Great Storm

Now, AS I HAVE SAID, WE CAME AT LAST IN SAFETY
to the open sea, and so for a time had some degree
of peace; though it was long ere we threw off all of
the terror which the Land of Lonesomeness had cast
over our hearts.

And one more matter there is regarding that land,
which my memory recalls. It will be remembered that
George found certain wrappers upon which there was
writing. Now, in the haste of our leaving, he had given
no thought to take them with him; yet a portion of one
he found within the side pocket of his jacket, and it
ran somewhat thus:—

"But I hear my lover's voice wailing in the night, and
I go to find him; for my loneliness is not to be borne.
May God have mercy upon me!"

And that was all.

For a day and a night we stood out from the land
towards the North, having a steady breeze to which we
set our lug sails, and so made very good way, the sea
being quiet, though with a slow, lumbering swell from
the Southward.

It was on the morning of the second day of our escape that we met with the beginnings of our adventure

into the Silent Sea, the which I am about to make so clear as I am able.

The night had been quiet, and the breeze steady until near on to the dawn, when the wind slacked away to nothing, and we lay there waiting, perchance the sun should bring the breeze with it. And this it did; but no such wind as we did desire; for when the morning came upon us, we discovered all that part of the sky to be full of a fiery redness, which presently spread away down to the South, so that an entire quarter of the heavens was, as it seemed to us, a mighty arc of blood-colored fire.

Now, at the sight of these omens, the bo'sun gave orders to prepare the boats for the storm which we had reason to expect, looking for it in the South, for it was from that direction that the swell came rolling upon us. With this intent, we roused out so much heavy canvas as the boats contained, for we had gotten a bolt and a half from the hulk in the creek; also the boat covers which we could lash down to the brass studs under the gunnels of the boats. Then, in each boat, we mounted the whaleback—which had been stowed along the tops of the thwarts—also its supports, lashing the same to the thwarts below the knees. Then we laid two lengths of the stout canvas the full length of the boat over the whaleback, overlapping and nailing them to the same, so that they sloped away down over the gunnels upon each side as though they had formed a roof to us. Here, whilst some stretched the canvas, nailing its lower edges to the gunnel, others were employed in lashing together the oars and the mast, and to this bundle they secured a considerable length of new three-and-a-half-inch hemp rope, which we had brought away from the hulk along with the canvas. This rope was then passed over the bows and in through the painter ring, and thence to the forrard thwarts, where it was made fast, and we gave attention to parcel it with odd strips of canvas against danger of chafe. And the same was done in both of the boats, for we could not put our trust in the painters, besides which they had not sufficient length to secure safe and easy riding.

Now by this time we had the canvas nailed down to the gunnel around our boat, after which we spread the boat-cover over it, lacing it down to the brass studs beneath the gunnel. And so we had all the boat covered in, save a place in the stern where a man might stand to wield the steering oar, for the boats were double bowed. And in each boat we made the same preparation, lashing all movable articles, and preparing to meet so great a storm as might well fill the heart with terror; for the sky cried out to us that it would be no light wind, and further, the great swell from the South grew more huge with every hour that passed; though as yet it was without virulence, being slow and oily and black against the redness of the sky.

Presently we were ready, and had cast over the bundle of oars and the mast, which was to serve as our sea-anchor, and so we lay waiting. It was at this time that the bo'sun called over to Josh certain advice with regard to that which lay before us. And after that the two of them sculled the boats a little apart; for there might be a danger of their being dashed together by the first violence of the storm.

And so came a time of waiting, with Josh and the bo'sun each of them at the steering oars, and the rest of us stowed away under the coverings. From where I crouched near the bo'sun, I had sight of Josh away upon our port side: he was standing up black as a shape of night against the mighty redness, when the boat came to the foamless crowns of the swells, and then gone from sight in the hollows between.

Now midday had come and gone, and we had made shift to eat so good a meal as our appetites would allow; for we had no knowledge how long it might be ere we should have chance of another, if, indeed, we had ever need to think more of such. And then, in the middle part of the afternoon, we heard the first cryings of the storm—a far-distant moaning, rising and falling most solemnly.

Presently, all the Southern part of the horizon so high up, maybe, as some seven to ten degrees, was blotted out by a great black wall of cloud, over which the red glare came down upon the great swells as though from the light of some vast and unseen fire. It was about this time, I observed that the sun had the appearance of a great full moon, being pale and clearly defined, and seeming to have no warmth nor brilliancy; and this, as may be imagined, seemed most strange to us, the more so because of the redness in the South and East.

And all this while the swells increased most prodigiously; though without making broken water: yet they informed us that we had done well to take so much precaution; for surely they were raised by a very great storm. A little before evening, the moaning came again, and then a space of silence; after which there rose a very sudden bellowing, as of wild beasts, and then once more the silence.

About this time, the bo'sun making no objection, I raised my head above the cover until I was in a standing position; for, until now, I had taken no more than occasional peeps; and I was very glad of the chance to stretch my limbs; for I had grown mightily cramped. Having stirred the sluggishness of my blood, I sat me down again; but in such position that I could see every part of the horizon without difficulty. Ahead of us, that is to the South, I saw now that the great wall of cloud had risen some further degrees, and there was something less of the redness; though, indeed, what there was left of it was sufficiently terrifying; for it appeared to crest the black cloud like red foam, seeming, it might be, as though a mighty sea made ready to break over the world.

Towards the West, the sun was sinking behind a curious red-tinted haze, which gave it the appearance of a dull red disk. To the North, seeming very high in the sky, were some flecks of cloud lying motionless, and of a very pretty rose color. And here I may remark that all the sea to the North of us appeared as a very ocean of dull red fire; though, as might be expected, the swells, coming up from the South, against the light were so many exceeding great hills of blackness.

It was just after I had made these observations that we heard again the distant roaring of the storm, and I know not how to convey the exceeding terror of that sound. It was as though some mighty beast growled far down towards the South; and it seemed to make very clear to me that we were but two small craft in a very lonesome place. Then, even while the roaring lasted, I saw a sudden light flare up, as it were from the edge of the Southern horizon. It had somewhat the appearance of lightning; yet vanished not immediately, as is the wont of lightning; and more, it had not been my experience to witness such spring up from out of the sea, but, rather, down from the heavens. Yet I have little doubt but that it was a form of lightning; for it came many times after this, so that I had chance to observe it minutely. And frequently, as I watched, the storm would shout at us in a most fearsome manner.

Then, when the sun was low upon the horizon, there came to our ears a very shrill, screaming noise, most penetrating and distressing, and, immediately afterwards the bo'sun shouted out something in a hoarse voice, and commenced to sway furiously upon the steering oar. I saw his stare fixed upon a point a little on our larboard bow, and perceived that in that direction the sea was all blown up into vast clouds of dust-like froth, and I knew that the storm was upon us. Immediately afterwards a cold blast struck us; but we suffered no harm, for the bo'sun had gotten the boat bows-on by this. The wind passed us, and there was an instant of calm. And now all the air above us was full of a continuous roaring, so very loud and intense that I was like to be deafened. To windward, I perceived an enormous wall of spray bearing down upon us, and I heard again the shrill screaming, pierce through the roaring. Then the bo'sun whipped in his oar under the cover, and, reaching forward, drew the canvas aft, so that it covered the entire boat, and he held it down against the gunnel upon the starboard side, shouting in my ear to do likewise upon the larboard. Now had it not been for this forethought on the part of the bo'sun we had been all dead men; and this may be the better believed when I explain that we felt the water falling upon the stout canvas overhead, tons and tons; though so beaten to froth as to lack solidity to sink or crush us. I have said "felt"; for I would make it so clear as may be, here once and for all, that so intense was the roaring and screaming of the elements, there could no sound have penetrated to us, no! not the pealing of mighty thunders. And so for the space of maybe a full minute the boat quivered and shook most vilely, so that she seemed like to have been shaken in pieces, and from a dozen places between the gunnel and the covering canvas, the water spurted in upon us. And here one other thing I would make mention of: During that minute, the boat had ceased to rise and fall upon the great swell, and whether this was because the sea was flattened by the first rush of the wind, or that the excess of the storm held her steady, I am unable to tell; and can put down only that which we felt.

Now, in a little, the first fury of the blast being spent, the boat began to sway from side to side, as though the wind blew now upon the one beam, and now upon the other; and several times we were stricken heavily with the blows of solid water. But presently this ceased, and we returned once again to the rise and fall of the swell, only that now we received a cruel jerk every time that the boat came upon the top of a sea. And so a while passed.

Towards midnight, as I should judge, there came

some mighty flames of lightning, so bright that they lit up the boat through the double covering of canvas; yet no man of us heard aught of the thunder; for the roaring of the storm made all else a silence.

And so to the dawn, after which, finding that we were still, by the mercy of God, possessed of our lives, we made shift to eat and drink; after which we slept.

Now, being extremely wearied by the stress of the past night, I slumbered through many hours of the storm, waking at some time between noon and evening. Overhead, as I lay looking upwards, the canvas showed of a dull leadenish color, blackened completely at whiles by the dash of spray and water. And so, presently, having eaten again, and feeling that all things lay in the hands of the Almighty, I came once more upon sleep.

Twice through the following night was I wakened by the boat being hurled upon her beam-ends by the blows of the seas; but she righted easily, and took scarce any water, the canvas proving a very roof of safety. And so the morning came again.

Being now rested, I crawled after to where the bo'sun lay, and, the noise of the storm lulling odd instants, shouted in his ear to know whether the wind was easing at whiles. To this he nodded, whereat I felt a most joyful sense of hope pulse through me, and ate such food as could be gotten, with a very good relish.

In the afternoon, the sun broke out suddenly, lighting up the boat most gloomily through the wet canvas; yet a very welcome light it was, and bred in us a hope that the storm was near to breaking. In a little, the sun disappeared; but, presently, it coming again, the bo'sun beckoned to me to assist him, and we removed such temporary nails as we had used to fasten down the after part of the canvas, and pushed back the covering a space sufficient to allow our heads to go through into the daylight. On looking out, I discovered the air to be full of spray, beaten as fine as dust, and then, before I could note aught else, a little gout of water took me in the face with such force as to deprive me of breath; so that I had to descend beneath the canvas for a little while.

So soon as I was recovered, I thrust forth my head again, and now I had some sight of the terrors around us. As each huge sea came towards us, the boat shot up to meet it, right up to its very crest, and there, for the space of some instants, we would seem to be swamped in a very ocean of foam, boiling up on each side of the boat to the height of many feet. Then, the sea passing from under us, we would go swooping dizzily down the great, black, froth-splotched back of the wave, until the oncoming sea caught us up most mightily. Odd whiles, the crest of a sea would hurl forward before we had reached the top, and though the boat shot upward like a veritable feather, yet the water would swirl right over us, and we would have to draw in our heads most suddenly; in such cases the wind flapping the cover down so soon as our hands were removed. And, apart from the way in which the boat met the seas, there was a very sense of terror in the air: the continuous roaring and howling of the storm; the *screaming* of the foam, as the frothy summits of the briny mountains hurled past us, and the wind that tore the breath out of our weak human throats, are things scarce to be conceived.

Presently, we drew in our heads, the sun having vanished again, and nailed down the canvas once more, and so prepared for the night.

From here on until the morning, I have very little knowledge of any happenings; for I slept much of the time, and, for the rest, there was little to know, cooped up beneath the cover. Nothing save the interminable, thundering swoop of the boat downwards, and then the halt and upward hurl, and the occasional plunges and surges to larboard or starboard, occasioned, I can only suppose, by the indiscriminate might of the seas.

I would make mention here, how that I had little thought all this while for the peril of the other boat, and, indeed, I was so very full of our own that it is no matter at which to wonder. However, as it proved, and as this is a most suitable place in which to tell it, the boat that held Josh and the rest of the crew came through the storm with safety; though it was not until many years afterwards that I had the good fortune to hear from Josh himself how that, after the storm, they were picked up by a homeward-bound vessel, and landed in the Port of London.

And now, to our own happenings.

VI: The Weed-Choked Sea

IT WAS SOME LITTLE WHILE BEFORE MIDDAY THAT we grew conscious that the sea had become very much less violent; and this despite the wind roaring with scarce abated noise. And, presently, everything about the boat, saving the wind, having grown indubitably calmer, and no great water breaking over the canvas, the bo'sun beckoned me again to assist him lift the after part of the cover. This we did, and put forth our heads to inquire the reason of the unexpected quietness of the sea; not knowing but that we had come suddenly under the lee of some unknown land. Yet, for a space, we could see nothing, beyond the surrounding billows; for the sea was still very furious, though no matter to cause us concern, after that through which we had come.

Presently, however, the bo'sun, raising himself, saw something, and, bending cried in my ear that there was a low bank which broke the force of the sea; but he was full of wonder to know how that we had passed it without shipwreck. And whilst he was still pondering the matter I raised myself, and took a look on all sides of us, and so I discovered that there lay another great bank upon our larboard side, and this I pointed out to him. Immediately afterwards, we came upon a great mass of seaweed swung up on the crest of a sea, and, presently, another. And so we drifted on, and the seas grew less with astonishing rapidity, so that, in a little, we stript off the cover so far as the midship thwart; for the rest of the men were sorely in need of the fresh air, after so long a time below the canvas covering.

It was after we had eaten, that one of them made out that there was another low bank astern upon which we were drifting. At that, the bo'sun stood up and made an examination of it, being much exercised in his mind to know how we might come clear of it with safety. Presently, however, we had come so near to it that we discovered it to be composed of seaweed, and so we let the boat drive upon it, making no doubt but that the other banks, which we had seen, were of a similar nature.

In a little, we had driven in among the weed; yet, though our speed was greatly slowed, we made some progress, and so in time came out upon the other side, and now we found the sea to be near quiet, so that we hauled in our sea anchor—which had collected a great mass of weed about it—and removed the whaleback and canvas coverings, after which we stepped the mast, and set a tiny storm-foresail upon the boat; for we wished to have her under control, and could set no more than this, because of the violence of the breeze.

Thus we drove on before the wind, the bo'sun steering, and avoiding all such banks as showed ahead, and ever the sea grew calmer. Then, when it was near on to evening, we discovered a huge stretch of the weed that seemed to block all the sea ahead, and, at that, we hauled down the foresail, and took to our oars, and began to pull, broadside on to it, towards the West. Yet so strong was the breeze, that we were being driven down rapidly upon it. And then, just before sunset, we opened out the end of it, and drew in our oars, very thankful to set the little foresail, and run off again before the wind.

And so, presently, the night came down upon us, and the bo'sun made us take turn and turn about to keep a look-out; for the boat was going some knots through the water, and we were among strange seas; but *he* took no sleep all that night, keeping always to the steering oar.

I have memory, during my time of watching, of passing odd floating masses, which I make no doubt were weed, and once we drove right atop of one; but drew clear without much trouble. And all the while, through the dark to starboard, I could make out the dim outline of that enormous weed extent lying low upon the sea, and seeming without end. And so, presently, my time to watch being at an end, I returned to my slumber, and when next I waked it was morning.

Now the morning discovered to me that there was no end to the weed upon our starboard side; for it stretched away into the distance ahead of us so far as we could see; while all about us the sea was full of floating masses of the stuff. And then, suddenly, one of the men cried out that there was a vessel in among the weed. At that, as may be imagined, we were very greatly excited, and stood upon the thwarts that we might get better view of her. Thus I saw her a great way in from the edge of the weed, and I noted that her foremast was gone near to the deck, and she had no main top-mast; though, strangely enough, her mizzen stood unharmed. And beyond this, I could make out but little, because of the distance; though the sun, which was upon our larboard side, gave me some sight of her hull, but not much, because of the weed in which she was deeply embedded; yet it seemed to me that her sides were very weather-worn, and in one place some glistening brown object, which may have been a fungus, caught the rays of the sun, sending off a wet sheen.

There we stood, all of us, upon the thwarts, staring and exchanging opinions, and were like to have overset the boat; but that the bo'sun ordered us down. And after this we made our breakfast, and had much discussion regarding the stranger, as we ate.

Later, towards midday, we were able to set our mizzen; for the storm had greatly modified, and so, presently, we hauled away to the West, to escape a great bank of the weed which ran out from the main body. Upon rounding this, we let the boat off again, and set the main lug, and thus made very good speed before the wind. Yet though we ran all that afternoon parallel with the weed to starboard, we came not to its end. And three separate times we saw the hulks of rotting vessels, some of them having the appearance of a previous age, so ancient did they seem.

Now, towards evening, the wind dropped to a very little breeze, so that we made but slow way, and thus we had better chance to study the weed. And now we saw that it was full of crabs; though for the most part so very minute as to escape the casual glance; yet they were not all small, for in a while I discovered a swaying among the weed, a little way in from the edge, and immediately I saw the mandible of a very great crab stir amid the weed. At that, hoping to obtain it for food, I pointed it out to the bo'sun, suggesting that we should try and capture it. And so, there being by now scarce any wind, he bade us get out a couple of the oars, and back the boat up to the weed. This we did, after which he made fast a piece of salt meat to a bit of spun yarn, and bent this on to the boat-hook. Then he made a running bowline, and slipped the loop on to the shaft of the boat-hook, after which he held out the boat-hook, after the fashion of a fishing-rod, over the place where I had seen the crab. Almost immediately, there swept up an enormous claw, and grasped the meat, and at that, the bo'sun cried out to me to take an oar and slide the bowline along the boat-hook, so that it should fall over the claw; and this I did, and immediately some of us hauled upon the line, taughtening it about the great claw. Then the bo'sun sung out to us to haul the crab aboard, that we had it most securely; yet on the instant we had reason to wish that we had been less successful; for the creature, feeling the tug of our pull upon it, tossed the weed in all directions, and thus we had full sight of it, and discovered it to be so great a crab as is scarce conceivable—a very monster. And further, it was apparent to us that the brute had no fear of us, nor intention to escape; but rather made to come at us; whereat the bo'sun, perceiving our danger, cut the line, and bade us put weight upon the oars, and so in a moment we were in safety, and very determined to have no more meddlings with such creatures.

Presently, the night came upon us, and, the wind remaining low, there was everywhere about us a great stillness, most solemn after the continuous roaring of the storm which had beset us in the previous days. Yet now and again a little wind would rise and blow across the sea, and where it met the weed, there would come a low, damp rustling, so that I could hear the passage of it for no little time after the calm had come once more all about us.

Now it is a strange thing that I, who had slept amid the noise of the past days, should find sleeplessness amid so much calm; yet so it was, and presently I took the steering oar, proposing that the rest should sleep, and to this the bo'sun agreed, first warning me, however, most particularly to have care that I kept the boat off the weed (for we had still a little way on us), and, further, to call him should anything unforeseen occur. And after that, almost immediately he fell asleep, as indeed did the most of the men.

From the time that I relieved the bo'sun, until midnight, I sat upon the gunnel of the boat, with the steering oar under my arm, and watched and listened, most full of a sense of the strangeness of the seas into which we had come. It is true that I had heard tell of seas choked up with weed—seas that were full of stagnation, having no tides; but I had not thought to come upon such an one in my wanderings; having, indeed, set down such tales as being bred of imagination, and without reality in fact.

Then, a little before the dawn, and when the sea was yet full of darkness, I was greatly startled to hear a prodigious splash amid the weed, mayhaps at a distance of some hundred yards from the boat. Then, as I stood full of alertness, and knowing not what the next moment might bring forth, there came to me across the immense waste of weed, a long, mournful cry, and then again the silence. Yet, though I kept very quiet, there came no further sound, and I was about to re-seat myself, when, afar off in that strange wilderness, there flashed out a sudden flame of fire.

Now upon seeing fire in the midst of so much lonesomeness, I was as one mazed, and could do naught but stare. Then, my judgment returning to me, I stooped and waked the bo'sun; for it seemed to me that this was a matter for his attention. He, after staring at it awhile, declared that he could see the shape of a vessel's hull beyond the flame; but, immediately, he was in doubt, as, indeed, I had been all the while. And then, even as we peered, the light vanished, and though we waited for the space of some minutes, watching steadfastly, there came no further sight of that strange illumination.

From now until the dawn, the bo'sun remained awake with me, and we talked much upon that which we had seen; yet could come to no satisfactory conclusion; for it seemed impossible to us that a place of so much desolation could contain any living being. And then, just as the dawn was upon us, there loomed up a fresh wonder—the hull of a great vessel maybe a couple or three score fathoms in from the edge of the weed. Now the wind was still very light, being no more than an occasional breath, so that we went past her at a drift; thus the dawn had strengthened sufficiently to give to us a clear sight of the stranger, before we had gone more than a little past her. And now I perceived that she lay full broadside on to us, and that her three masts were gone close down to the deck. Her side was streaked in places with rust, and in others a green scum overspread her; but it was no more than a glance that I gave at any of those matters; for I had spied something which drew all my attention—great leathery arms splayed all across her side, some of them crooked inboard over the rail, and then, low down, seen just above the weed, the huge, brown, glistening bulk of so great a monster as ever I had conceived. The bo'sun saw it in the same instant and cried out in a hoarse whisper that it was a mighty devil-fish, and then, even as he spoke, two of the arms flickered up into the cold light of the dawn, as though the creature had been asleep, and we had waked it. At that, the bo'sun seized an oar, and I did likewise, and, so swiftly as we dared, for fear of making any unneedful noise, we pulled the boat to a safer distance. From there and until the vessel had become indistinct by reason of the space we put between us, we watched that great creature clutched to the old hull, as it might be a limpet to a rock.

Presently, when it was broad day, some of the men began to rouse up, and in a little we broke our fast, which was not displeasing to me, who had spent the night watching. And so through the day we sailed with a very light wind upon our larboard quarter. And all the while we kept the great waste of weed upon our starboard side, and apart from the mainland of the weed, as it were, there were scattered about an uncountable number of weed islets and banks, and there were thin patches of it that appeared scarce above the water, and through these later we let the boat sail; for they had not sufficient density to impede our progress more than a little.

And then, when the day was far spent, we came in sight of another wreck amid the weeds. She lay in from the edge perhaps so much as the half of a mile, and

she had all three of her lower masts in, and her lower
yards squared. But what took our eyes more than aught
else was a great superstructure which had been built
upward from her rails, almost half-way to her main
tops, and this, as we were able to perceive, was sup-
ported by ropes let down from the yards; but of what
material the superstructure was composed, I have no
knowledge; for it was so over-grown with some form of
green stuff—as was so much of the hull as showed
above the weed—as to defy our guesses. And because
of this growth, it was borne upon us that the ship must
have been lost to the world a very great age ago. At this
suggestion, I grew full of solemn thought; for it
seemed to me that we had come upon the cemetery of
the oceans.

Now, in a little while after we had passed this ancient
craft, the night came down upon us, and we prepared
for sleep, and because the boat was making some little
way through the water, the bo'sun gave out that each of
us should stand our turn at the steering-oar, and that
he was to be called should any fresh matter transpire.
And so we settled down for the night, and owing to my
previous sleeplessness, I was full weary, so that I knew
nothing until the one whom I was to relieve shook me
into wakefulness. So soon as I was fully waked, I perceived that a low moon hung above the horizon, and
shed a very ghostly light across the great weed world to
starboard. For the rest, the night was exceeding quiet,
so that no sound came to me in all that ocean, save the
rippling of the water upon our bends as the boat
forged slowly along. And so I settled down to pass the
time ere I should be allowed to sleep; but first I asked
the man whom I had relieved, how long a time had
passed since moon-rise; to which he replied that it was
no more than the half of an hour, and after that I
questioned whether he had seen aught strange amid the
weed during his time at the oar; but he had seen nothing, except that once he had fancied a light had shown

in the midst of the waste; yet it could have been naught save a humor of the imagination; though apart from this, he had heard a strange crying a little after midnight, and twice there had been great splashes among the weed. And after that he fell asleep, being impatient at my questioning.

Now it so chanced that my watch had come just before the dawn; for which I was full of thankfulness, being in that frame of mind when the dark breeds strange and unwholesome fancies. Yet, though I was so near to the dawn, I was not to escape free of the dree influence of that place; for, as I sat, running my gaze to and fro over its grey immensity, it came to me that there were strange movements among the weed, and I seemed to see vaguely, as one may see things in dreams, dim white faces peer out at me here and there; yet my commonsense assured me that I was but deceived by the uncertain light and the sleep in my eyes; yet for all that, it put my nerves on the quiver.

A little later, there came to my ears the noise of a very great splash amid the weed; but though I stared with intentness, I could nowhere discern aught as likely to be the cause thereof. And then, suddenly, between me and the moon, there drove up from out of that great waste a vast bulk, flinging huge masses of weed in all directions. It seemed to be no more than a hundred fathoms distant, and, against the moon, I saw the outline of it most clearly—a mighty devil-fish. Then it had fallen back once more with a prodigious splash, and so the quiet fell again, finding me sore afraid, and no little bewildered that so monstrous a creature could leap with such agility. And then (in my fright I had let the boat come near to the edge of the weed) there came a subtle stir opposite to our starboard bow, and something slid down into the water. I swayed upon the oar to turn the boat's head outward, and with the same movement leant forward and sideways to peer, bringing my face near to the boat's rail. In the same instant, I found myself looking down into a white demoniac face, human save that the mouth and nose had greatly the appearance of a beak. The thing was gripping at the side of the boat with two flickering hands—gripping the bare, smooth outer surface, in a way that woke in my mind a sudden memory of the great devil-fish which had clung to the side of the wreck we had passed in the previous dawn. I saw the face come up towards me, and one misshapen hand fluttered almost to my throat, and there came a sudden, hateful reek in my nostrils—foul and abominable. Then, I came into possession of my faculties, and drew back with great haste and a wild cry of fear. And then I had the steering-oar by the middle, and was smiting downward with the loom over the side of the boat; but the thing was gone from my sight. I remember shouting out to the bo'sun and to the men to awake, and then the bo'sun had me by the shoulder, was calling in my ear to know what dire thing had come about. At that, I cried out that I did not know, and, presently, being somewhat calmer, I told them of the thing that I had seen; but even as I told of it, there seemed to be no truth in it, so that they were all at a loss to know whether I had fallen asleep, or that I had indeed seen a devil.

And presently the dawn was upon us.

VII: The Island in the Weed

IT WAS AS WE WERE ALL DISCUSSING THE MATTER
of the devil face that had peered up at me out of the
water, that Job, the ordinary seaman, discovered the island in the light of the growing dawn, and, seeing it,
sprang to his feet, with so loud a cry that we were
like for the moment to have thought he had seen a
second demon. Yet when we made discovery of that
which he had already perceived, we checked our blame
at his sudden shout; for the sight of land, after so
much desolation, made us very warm in our hearts.

Now at first the island seemed but a very small matter; for we did not know at that time that we viewed it
from its end; yet despite this, we took to our oars and
rowed with all haste towards it, and so, coming nearer,
were able to see that it had a greater size than we had
imagined. Presently, having cleared the end of it, and
keeping to that side which was further from the great
mass of the weed-continent, we opened out a bay that
curved inward to a sandy beach, most seductive to our
tired eyes. Here, for the space of a minute, we paused
to survey the prospect, and I saw that the island was of
a very strange shape, having a great hump of black
rock at either end, and dipping down into a steep valley
between them. In this valley there seemed to be a deal

of a strange vegetation that had the appearance of mighty toadstools; and down nearer the beach there was a thick grove of a kind of very tall reed, and these we discovered afterwards to be exceeding tough and light, having something of the qualities of the bamboo.

Regarding the beach, it might have been most reasonably supposed that it would be very thick with the driftweed; but this was not so, at least, not at that time; though a projecting horn of the black rock which ran out into the sea from the upper end of the island, was thick with it.

And now, the bo'sun having assured himself that there was no appearance of any danger, we bent to our oars, and presently had the boat aground upon the beach, and here, finding it convenient, we made our breakfast. During this meal, the bo'sun discussed with us the most proper thing to do, and it was decided to push the boat off from the shore, leaving Job in her, whilst the remainder of us made some exploration of the island.

And so, having made an end of eating, we proceeded as we had determined, leaving Job in the boat, ready to scull ashore for us if we were pursued by any savage creature, while the rest of us made our way towards the nearer hump, from which, as it stood some hundred feet above the sea, we hoped to get a very good idea of the remainder of the island. First, however, the bo'sun handed out to us the two cutlasses and the cut-and-thrust (the other two cutlasses being in Josh's boat), and, taking one himself, he passed me the cut-and-thrust, and gave the other cutlass to the biggest of the men. Then he bade the others keep their sheath-knives handy, and was proceeding to lead the way, when one of them called out to us to wait a moment, and, with that, ran quickly to the clump of reeds. Here, he took one with both his hands and bent upon it; but it would not break, so that he had to notch it about with his knife, and thus, in a little, he had it clear. After this, he cut off the upper part, which was too thin and lissom for his purpose, and then thrust the handle of his knife into the end of the portion which he had retained, and in this wise he had a most serviceable lance or spear. For the reeds were very strong, and hollow after the fashion of bamboo, and when he had bound some yarn about the end into which he had thrust his knife, so as to prevent it splitting, it was a fit enough weapon for any man.

Now the bo'sun, perceiving the happiness of the fellow's idea, bade the rest make to themselves similar weapons, and whilst they were busy thus, he commended the man very warmly. And so, in a little, being now most comfortably armed, we made inland towards the nearer black hill, in very good spirits. Presently, we were come to the rock which formed the hill, and found that it came up out of the sand with great abruptness, so that we could not climb it on the seaward side. At that, the bo'sun led us round a space towards that side where lay the valley, and here there was under-foot neither sand nor rock; but ground of strange and spongy texture, and then suddenly, rounding a jutting spur of the rock, we came upon the first of the vegetation—an incredible mushroom; nay, I should say toadstool; for it had no healthy look about it, and gave out a heavy, mouldy odor. And now we perceived that the valley was filled with them, all, that is, save a great circular patch where nothing appeared to be growing; though we were not yet at a sufficient height to ascertain the reason of this.

Presently, we came to a place where the rock was split by a great fissure running up to the top, and showing many ledges and convenient shelves upon which we might obtain hold and footing. And so we set-to about climbing, helping one another so far as we had ability, until, in about the space of some ten minutes, we reached the top, and from thence had a very fine view. We perceived now that there was a beach upon that side of the island which was opposed to the weed; though, unlike that upon which we had landed, it was greatly choked with weed which had drifted ashore. After that, I gave notice to see what space of water lay between the island and the edge of the great weed-continent, and guessed it to be no more than maybe some ninety yards, at which I fell to wishing that it had been greater, for I was grown much in awe of the weed and the strange things which I conceived it to contain.

Abruptly, the bo'sun clapped me upon the shoulder, and pointed to some object that lay out in the weed at a distance of not much less than the half of a mile from where we stood. Now, at first, I could not conceive what manner of thing it was at which I stared, until the bo'sun, remarking my bewilderment, informed me that it was a vessel all covered in, no doubt as a protection against the devil-fish and other strange creatures in the weed. And now I began to trace the hull of her amid all that hideous growth; but of her masts, I could discern nothing; and I doubted not but that they had been carried away by some storm ere she was caught by the weed; and then the thought came to me of the end of those who had built up that protection against the horrors which the weed-world held hidden amid its slime.

Presently, I turned my gaze once more upon the island, which was very plain to see from where we stood. I conceived, now that I could see so much of it, that its length would be near to half a mile, though its breadth was something under four hundred yards; thus it was very long in proportion to its width. In the middle part it had less breadth than at the ends, being perhaps three hundred yards at its narrowest, and a hundred yards wider at its broadest.

Upon both sides of the island, as I have made already a mention, there was a beach, though this extended no great distance along the shore, the remainder being composed of the black rock of which the hills were formed. And now, having a closer regard to the beach upon the weed-side of the island, I discovered amid the wrack that had been cast ashore, a portion of the lower mast and topmast of some great ship, with rigging attached; but the yards were all gone. This find, I pointed out to the bo'sun, remarking that it might prove of use for firing; but he smiled at me, telling me that the dried weed would make a very abundant fire, and this without going to the labor of cutting the mast into suitable logs.

And now, he, in turn, called my attention to the place where the huge fungi had come to a stop in their growing, and I saw that in the centre of the valley there was a great circular opening in the earth, like to the mouth of a prodigious pit, and it appeared to be filled to within a few feet of the mouth with water, over which spread a brown and horrid scum. Now, as may be supposed, I stared with some intentness at this; for it had the look of having been made with labor, being very symmetrical; yet I could not conceive but that I was deluded by the distance, and that it would have a rougher appearance when viewed from a nearer standpoint.

From contemplating this, I looked down upon the little bay in which our boat floated. Job was sitting in the stern, sculling gently with the steering oar and watching us. At that, I waved my hand to him in friendly fashion, and he waved back, and then, even as I looked, I saw something in the water under the boat —something dark colored that was all of a-move. The boat appeared to be floating over it as over a mass of sunk weed, and then I saw that, whatever it was, it was rising to the surface. At this a sudden horror came over me, and I clutched the bo'sun by the arm, and pointed, crying out that there was something under the boat. Now the bo'sun, so soon as he saw the thing, ran forward to the brow of the hill and, placing his hands to his mouth after the fashion of a trumpet, sang out to the boy to bring the boat to the shore and make fast the painter to a large piece of rock. At the bo'sun's hail, the lad called out "I, I," and, standing up, gave a sweep with his oar that brought the boat's head round towards the beach. Fortunately for him he was no more than some thirty yards from the shore at this time, else he had never come to it in this life; for the next moment the moving brown mass beneath the boat shot out a great tentacle and the oar was torn out of Job's hands with such power as to throw him right over on to the starboard gunnel of the boat. The oar itself was drawn down out of sight, and for the minute the boat was left untouched. Now the bo'sun cried out to the boy to take another oar, and get ashore while still he had chance, and at that we all called out various things, one advising one thing, and another recommending some other; yet our advice was vain, for the boy moved not, at which some cried out that he was stunned. I looked now to where the brown thing had been, for the boat had moved a few fathoms from the spot, having got some way upon her before the oar was snatched, and thus I discovered that the monster had disappeared, having, I conceived, sunk again into the depths from which it had risen; yet it might re-appear at any moment, and in that case the boy would be taken before our eyes.

At this juncture, the bo'sun called to us to follow him, and led the way to the great fissure up which we had climbed, and so, in a minute, we were, each of us, scrambling down with what haste we could make towards the valley. And all the while as I dropped from ledge to ledge, I was full of torment to know whether the monster had returned.

The bo'sun was the first man to reach the bottom of the cleft, and he set off immediately round the base of the rock to the beach, the rest of us following him as we made safe our footing in the valley. I was the third man down; but, being light and fleet of foot, I passed the second man and caught up with the bo'sun just as he came upon the sand. Here, I found that the boat was within some five fathoms of the beach, and I could see Job still lying insensible; but of the monster there was no sign.

And so matters were, the boat nearly a dozen yards from the shore, and Job lying insensible in her; with, somewhere near under her keel (for all that we knew) a great monster, and we helpless upon the beach.

Now I could not imagine how to save the lad, and indeed I fear he had been left to destruction—for I had deemed it madness to try to reach the boat by swimming—but for the extraordinary bravery of the bo'sun, who, without hesitating, dashed into the water and swam boldly out to the boat, which, by the grace of God, he reached without mishap, and climbed in over the bows. Immediately, he took the painter and hove it to us, bidding us tail on to it and bring the boat to shore without delay, and by this method of gaining the beach he showed wisdom; for in this wise he escaped attracting the attention of the monster by unneedful stirring of the water, as he would surely have done had he made use of an oar.

Yet, despite his care, we had not finished with the creature; for, just as the boat grounded, I saw the lost steering oar shoot up half its length out of the sea, and immediately there was a mighty splather in the water astern, and the next instant the air seemed full of huge, whirling arms. At that, the bo'sun gave one look behind, and, seeing the thing upon him, snatched the boy into his arms, and sprang over the bows on to the sand. Now, at sight of the devil-fish, we had all made for the back of the beach at a run, none troubling even to retain the painter, and because of this, we were like to have lost the boat; for the great cuttle-fish had its arms all splayed about it, seeming to have a mind to drag it down into the deep water from whence it had risen, and it had possibly succeeded, but that the bo'sun brought us all to our senses; for, having laid Job out of harm's way, he was the first to seize the painter, which lay trailed upon the sand, and, at that, we got back our courage and ran to assist him.

Now there happened to be convenient a great spike of rock, the same, indeed, to which the bo'sun had bidden Job tie the boat, and to this we ran the painter, taking a couple of turns about it and two half-hitches, and now, unless the rope carried away, we had no reason to fear the loss of the boat; though there seemed to us to be a danger of the creature's crushing it. Because of this, and because of a feeling of natural anger against the thing, the bo'sun took up from the sand one of the spears which had been cast down when we hauled the boat ashore. With this, he went down so far as seemed safe, and prodded the creature in one of its tentacles— the weapon entering easily, at which I was surprised, for I had understood that these monsters were near to invulnerable in all parts save their eyes. At receiving this stab, the great fish appeared to feel no hurt for it showed no signs of pain, and, at that, the bo'sun was further emboldened to go nearer, so that he might deliver a more deadly wound; yet scarce had he taken two steps before the hideous thing was upon him, and, but for an agility wonderful in so great a man, he had been destroyed. Yet, spite of so narrow an escape from death, he was not the less determined to wound or destroy the creature, and, to this end, he despatched some of us to the grove of reeds to get half a dozen of the strongest, and when we returned with these, he bade two of the men lash their spears securely to them, and by this means they had now spears of a length of between thirty and forty feet. With these, it was possible to attack the devil-fish without coming within reach of its tentacles. And now being ready, he took one of the spears, telling the biggest of the men to take the other. Then he directed him to aim for the right eye of the huge fish whilst he would attack the left.

Now since the creature had so nearly captured the

bo'sun, it had ceased to tug at the boat, and lay silent, with its tentacles spread all about it, and its great eyes appearing just over the stern, so that it presented an appearance of watching our movements; though I doubt if it saw us with any clearness; for it must have been dazed with the brightness of the sunshine.

And now the bo'sun gave the signal to attack, at which he and the man ran down upon the creature with their lances, as it were, in rest. The bo'sun's spear took the monster truly in its left eye; but the one wielded by the men was too bendable, and sagged so much that it struck the stern-post of the boat, the knifeblade snapping off short. Yet it mattered not; for the wound inflicted by the bo'sun's weapon was so frightful, that the giant cuttle-fish released the boat, and slid back into deep water, churning it into foam, and gouting blood.

For some minutes we waited to make sure that the monster had indeed gone, and after that, we hastened to the boat, and drew her up so far as we were able; after which we unloaded the heaviest of her contents, and so were able to get her right clear of the water.

And for an hour afterwards the sea all about the little beach was stained black, and in places red.

VIII: The Noises in the Valley

Now, so soon as we had gotten the boat into safety, the which we did with a most feverish haste, the bo'sun gave his attention to Job; for the boy had not yet recovered from the blow which the loom of the oar had dealt him beneath the chin when the monster snatched at it. For awhile, his attentions produced no effect; but presently, having bathed the lad's face with water from the sea, and rubbed rum into his breast over the heart, the youth began to show signs of life, and soon opened his eyes, whereupon the bo'sun gave him a stiff jorum of the rum, after which he asked him how he seemed in himself. To this Job replied in a weak voice that he was dizzy and his head and neck ached badly; on hearing which, the bo'sun bade him keep lying until he had come more to himself. And so we left him in quietness under a little shade of canvas and reeds; for the air was warm and the sand dry, and he was not like to come to any harm there.

At at little distance, under the directing of the bo'sun, we made to prepare dinner; for we were now very hungry, it seeming a great while since we had broken our fast. To this end, the bo'sun sent two of the men across the island to gather some of the dry seaweed; for we intended to cook some of the salt meat, this being the first cooked meal since ending the meat which we had boiled before leaving the ship in the creek.

In the meanwhile, and until the return of the men with the fuel, the bo'sun kept us busied in various ways. Two he sent to cut a faggot of the reeds, and another couple to bring the meat and the iron boiler, the latter being one that we had taken from the old brig.

Presently, the men returned with the dried seaweed, and very curious stuff it seemed, some of it being in chunks near as thick as a man's body; but exceeding brittle by reason of its dryness. And so in a little, we had a very good fire going, which we fed with the seaweed and pieces of the reeds; though we found the latter to be but indifferent fuel, having too much sap, and being troublesome to break into convenient size.

Now when the fire had grown red and hot, the bo'sun half filled the boiler with sea water, in which he placed the meat; and the pan, having a stout lid, he did not scruple to place it in the very heart of the fire, so that soon we had the contents boiling merrily.

Having gotten the dinner under way, the bo'sun set about preparing our camp for the night, which we did by making a rough framework with the reeds, over which we spread the boat's sails and the cover, pegging the canvas down with tough splinters of the reed. When this was completed, we set-to and carried there all our stores, after which the bo'sun took us over to the other side of the island to gather fuel for the night, which we did, each man bearing a great double armful.

Now by the time that we had brought over, each of us, two loads of the fuel, we found the meat to be cooked, and so, without more to-do, set ourselves down and made a very good meal off it and some biscuits, after which we had each of us a sound tot of the rum. Having made an end of eating and drinking, the bo'sun went over to where Job lay, to inquire how he felt, and found him lying very quiet, though his breathing had

a heavy touch about it. However, we could conceive of
nothing by which he might be bettered, and so left him,
being more hopeful that Nature would bring him to
health than any skill of which we were possessed.

By this time it was late afternoon, so that the bo'sun
declared we might please ourselves until sunset, deem-
ing that we had earned a very good right to rest; but
that from sunset till the dawn we should, he told us,
have each of us to take turn and turn about to watch;
for though we were no longer upon the water, none
might say whether we were out of danger or not, as
witness the happening of the morning; though, certainly, he apprehended no danger from the devil-fish so
long as we kept well away from the water's edge.

And so from now until dark most of the men slept;
but the bo'sun spent much of that time in overhauling
the boat, to see how it might chance to have suffered
during the storm, and also whether the struggles of the
devil-fish had strained it in any way. And, indeed, it
was speedily evident that the boat would need some
attention; for the plank in her bottom next but one to
the keel, upon the starboard side, had been burst in-
wards; this having been done, it would seem, by some
rock in the beach hidden just beneath the water's edge,
the devil-fish having, no doubt, ground the boat down
upon it. Happily, the damage was not great; though it
would most certainly have to be carefully repaired before the boat would be again seaworthy. For the rest,
there seemed to be no other part needing attention.

Now I had not felt any call to sleep, and so had
followed the bo'sun to the boat, giving him a hand to
remove the bottom-boards, and finally to slue her bottom a little upwards, so that he might examine the leak
more closely. When he had made an end with the boat,
he went over to the stores, and looked closely into
their condition, and also to see how they were lasting.
And, after that, he sounded all the water-breakers;
having done which, he remarked that it would be well

for us if we could discover any fresh water upon the island.

By this time it was getting on towards evening, and the bo'sun went across to look at Job, finding him much as he had been when we visited him after dinner. At that, the bo'sun asked me to bring across one of the longer of the bottom-boards, which I did, and we made use of it as a stretcher to carry the lad into the tent. And afterwards, we carried all the loose woodwork of the boat into the tent, emptying the lockers of their contents, which included some oakum, a small boat's hatchet, a coil of one-and-a-half-inch hemp line, a good saw, an empty, colza-oil tin, a bag of copper nails, some bolts and washers, two fishing-lines, three spare tholes, a three-pronged grain without the shaft, two balls of spun yarn, three hanks of roping-twine, a piece of canvas with four roping-needles stuck in it, the boat's lamp, a spare plug, and a roll of light duck for making boat's sails.

And so, presently, the dark came down upon the island, at which had bo'sun waked the men, and bade them throw more fuel on to the fire, which had burned down to a mound of glowing embers much shrouded in ash. After that, one of them part filled the boiler with fresh water, and soon we were occupied most pleasantly upon a supper of cold, boiled salt-meat, hard biscuits, and rum mixed with hot water. During supper, the bo'sun made clear to the men regarding the watches, arranging how they should follow, so that I found I was set down to take my turn from midnight until one of the clock. Then, he explained to them about the burst plank in the bottom of the boat, and how that it would have to be put right before we could hope to leave the island, and that after that night we should have to go most strictly with the victuals; for there seemed to be nothing upon the island, that we had up till then discovered, fit to satisfy our bellies. More than this, if we could find no fresh water, he should have to distil some to make up for that which we had drunk, and this must be done before leaving the island.

Now by the time that the bo'sun had made an end of explaining these matters, we had ceased from eating, and soon after this we made each one of us a comfortable place in the sand within the tent, and lay down to sleep. For a while, I found myself very wakeful, which may have been because of the warmth of the night, and, indeed, at last, I got up and went out of the tent, conceiving that I might the better find sleep in the open air. And so it proved; for, having lain down at the side of the tent, a little way from the fire, I fell soon into a deep slumber, which at first was dreamless. Presently, however, I came upon a very strange and unsettling dream; for I dreamed that I had been left alone on the island, and was sitting very desolate upon the edge of the brown-scummed pit. Then I was aware suddenly that it was very dark and very silent, and I began to shiver; for it seemed to me that something which repulsed my whole being had come quietly behind me. At that I tried mightily to turn and look into the shadows among the great fungi that stood all about me; but I had no power to turn. And the thing was coming nearer, though never a sound came to me, and I gave out a scream, or tried to; but my voice made no stir in the rounding quiet; and then something wet and cold touched my face, and slithered down and covered my mouth, and paused there for a vile, breathless moment. It passed onward and fell to my throat—and stayed there. . . .

Some one stumbled and fell over my feet, and at that, I was suddenly awake. It was the man on watch taking a walk round the back of the tent, and he had not known of my presence till he fell over my boots. He was somewhat shaken and startled, as might be supposed; but steadied himself on learning that it was no wild creature crouched there in the shadow; and all the time, as I answered his inquiries, I was full of a strange, horrid feeling that something had left me at the moment of my awakening. There was a slight, hateful odour in my nostrils that was not altogether unfamiliar, and then, suddenly, I was aware that my face was damp and that there was a curious sense of tingling at my throat. I put up my hand and felt my face, and the hand when I brought it away was slippery with slime, and at that, I put up my other hand, and touched my throat, and there it was the same, only, in addition, there was a slight swelled place a little to one side of the wind-pipe, the sort of place that the bite of a mosquito will make; but I had no thought to blame any mosquito.

Now the stumbling of the man over me, my awakening, and the discovery that my face and throat were be-slimed, were but the happenings of some few, short instants; and then I was upon my feet, and following him round to the fire; for I had a sense of chilliness and a great desire not to be alone. Now, having come to the fire, I took some of the water that had been left in the boiler, and washed my face and neck, after which I felt more my own man. Then I asked the man to look at my throat, so that he might give me some idea of what manner of place the swelling seemed, and he, lighting a piece of the dry seaweed to act as a torch, made examination of my neck; but could see little, save a number of small ring-like marks, red inwardly, and white at the edges, and one of them was bleeding slightly. After that, I asked him whether he had seen anything moving round the tent; but he had seen nothing during all the time that he had been on watch; though it was true that he had heard odd noises; but nothing very near at hand. Of the places on my throat he seemed to think but little, suggesting that I had been bitten by some sort of sand-fly; but at that, I shook my head, and told him of my dream, and after that, he was as anxious to keep near me as I to him. And so the night passed onward, until my turn came to watch.

For a little while, the man whom I had relieved sat beside me; having, I conceived, the kindly intent of keeping me company; but so soon as I perceived this, I entreated him to go and get his sleep, assuring him that I had no longer any feelings of fear—such as had been mine upon awakening and discovering the state of my face and throat—; and, upon this, he consented to leave me, and so, in a little, I sat alone beside the fire.

For a certain space, I kept very quiet, listening; but no sound came to me out of the surrounding darkness, and so, as though it were a fresh thing, it was borne in upon me how that we were in a very abominable place of lonesomeness and desolation. And I grew very solemn.

Thus as I sat, the fire, which had not been replenished for a while, dwindled steadily until it gave but a dullish glow around. And then, in the direction of the valley, I heard suddenly the sound of a dull thud, the noise coming to me through the stillness with a very startling clearness. At that, I perceived that I was not doing my duty to the rest, nor to myself, by sitting and allowing the fire to cease from flaming; and immediately reproaching myself, I seized and cast a mass of the dry weed upon the fire, so that a great blaze shot up into the night, and afterwards I glanced quickly to right and to left, holding my cut-and-thrust very readily, and most thankful to the Almighty that I had brought no harm to any by reason of my carelessness, which I incline me to believe was that strange inertia which is bred by fear. And then, even as I looked about me, there came to me across the silence of the beach a fresh noise, a continual soft slithering to and fro in the bottom of the valley, as though a multitude of creatures moved stealthily. At this, I threw yet more fuel upon the fire, and after that I fixed my gaze in the direction of the valley: thus in the following instant it seemed to me that I saw a certain thing, as it might be a shadow, move on the outer borders of the firelight. Now the man who had kept watch before me had left his spear stuck upright in the sand convenient to my grasp, and, seeing something moving, I seized the weapon and hurled it with all my strength in its direction; but there came no answering cry to tell that I had struck anything living, and immediately afterwards there fell once more a great silence upon the island, being broken only by a far splash out upon the weed.

It may be conceived with truth that the above happenings had put a very considerable strain upon my nerves, so that I looked to and fro continually, with ever and anon a quick glance behind me; for it seemed to me that I might expect some demoniac creature to rush upon me at any moment. Yet, for the space of many minutes, there came to me neither any sight nor sound of living creature; so that I knew not what to think, being near to doubting if I had heard aught beyond the common.

And then, even as I made halt upon the threshold of doubt, I was assured that I had not been mistaken; for, abruptly, I was aware that all the valley was full of a rustling, scampering sort of noise, through which there came to me occasional soft thuds, and anon the former slithering sounds. And at that, thinking a host of evil things to be upon us, I cried out to the bo'sun and the men to awake.

Immediately upon my shout, the bo'sun rushed out from the tent, the men following, and every one with his weapon, save the man who had left his spear in the sand, and that lay now somewhere beyond the light of the fire. Then the bo'sun shouted, to know what thing had caused me to cry out; but I replied nothing, only held up my hand for quietness, yet when this was granted, the noises in the valley had ceased; so that the bo'sun turned to me, being in need of some explanation; but I begged him to hark a little longer, which he did, and, the sounds re-commencing almost immediately, he heard sufficient to know that I had not waked them all without due cause. And then, as we stood each one of us staring into the darkness where lay the valley, I seemed to see again some shadowy thing upon the boundary of the firelight; and, in the same instant, one of the men cried out and cast his spear into the darkness. But the bo'sun turned upon him with a very great anger; for in throwing his weapon, the man had left himself without, and thus brought danger to the whole; yet, as will be remembered, I had done likewise but a little since.

Presently, there coming again a quietness within the valley, and none knowing what might be toward, the bo'sun caught up a mass of the dry weed, and, lighting it at the fire, ran with it towards that portion of the beach which lay between us and the valley. Here he cast it upon the sand, singing out to some of the men to bring more of the weed, so that we might have a fire there, and thus be able to see if anything made to come at us out of the deepness of the hollow.

Presently, we had a very good fire, and by the light of this the two spears were discovered, both of them stuck in the sand, and no more than a yard one from the other, which seemed to me a very strange thing.

Now, for a while after the lighting of the second fire, there came no further sounds from the direction of the valley; nothing indeed to break the quietness of the island, save the occasional lonely splashes that sounded from time to time out in the vastness of the weed-continent. Then, about an hour after I had waked the bo'sun, one of the men who had been tending the fires came up to him to say that we had come to the end of our supply of weed-fuel. At that, the bo'sun looked very blank, the which did the rest of us, as well we might; yet there was no help for it, until one of the men bethought him of the remainder of the faggot of reeds which we had cut, and which, burning but poorly, we had discarded for the weed. This was discovered at the back of the tent, and with it we fed the fire that burned between us and the valley; but the other we suffered to die out, for the reeds were not sufficient to support even the one until the dawn.

At last, and whilst it was still dark, we came to the end of our fuel, and as the fire died down, so did the noises in the valley re-commence. And there we stood in the growing dark, each one keeping a very ready weapon, and a more ready glance. And at times the island would be mightily quiet, and then again the sounds of things crawling in the valley. Yet, I think the silences tried us the more.

And so at last came the dawn.

IX: What Happened in the Dusk

NOW WITH THE COMING OF THE DAWN, A LASTING
silence stole across the island and into the valley, and,
conceiving that we had nothing more to fear, the bo'sun
bade us get some rest, whilst he kept watch. And so I
got at last a very substantial little spell of sleep, which
made me fit enough for the day's work.

Presently, after some hours had passed, the bo'sun
roused us to go with him to the further side of the
island to gather fuel, and soon we were back with each
a load, so that in a little we had the fire going right
merrily.

Now for breakfast, we had a hash of broken biscuit,
salt meat and some shell-fish which the bo'sun had
picked up from the beach at the foot of the further
hill; the whole being right liberally flavoured with some
of the vinegar, which the bo'sun said would help keep
down any scurvy that might be threatening us. And at
the end of the meal he served out to us each a little of
the molasses, which we mixed with hot water, and
drank.

The meal being ended, he went into the tent to take
a look at Job, the which he had done already in the
early morning; for the condition of the lad preyed
somewhat upon him; he being, for all his size and top-

roughness, a man of surprisingly tender heart. Yet the boy remained much as on the previous evening, so that we knew not what to do with him to bring him into better health. One thing we tried, knowing that no food had passed his lips since the previous morning, and that was to get some little quantity of hot water, rum and molasses down his throat; for it seemed to us he might die from very lack of food; but though we worked with him for more than the half of an hour, we could not get him to come-to sufficiently to take anything, and without that we had fear of suffocating him. And so, presently, we had perforce to leave him within the tent, and go about our business; for there was very much to be done.

Yet, before we did aught else, the bo'sun led us all into the valley, being determined to make a very thorough exploration of it, perchance there might be any lurking beast or devil-thing waiting to rush out and destroy us as we worked, and more, he would make search that he might discover what manner of creatures had disturbed our night.

Now in the early morning, when we had gone for the fuel, we had kept to the upper skirt of the valley where the rock of the nearer hill came down into the spongy ground; but now we struck right down into the middle part of the vale, making a way amid the mighty fungi to the pit-like opening that filled the bottom of the valley. Now though the ground was very soft, there was in it so much of springiness that it left no trace of our steps after we had gone on a little way, none, that is, save that in odd places, a wet patch followed upon our treading. Then, when we got ourselves near to the pit, the ground became softer, so that our feet sank into it, and left very real impressions; and here we found tracks most curious and bewildering; for amid the slush edged the pit—which I would mention here had less the look of a pit now that I had come near to it—were multitudes of markings which I can liken to nothing so much as the tracks of mighty slugs amid the mud, only that they were not altogether like to that of slugs'; for there were other markings such as might have been made by bunches of eels cast down and picked up continually, at least, this is what they suggested to me, and I do but put it down as such.

Apart from the markings which I have mentioned, there was everywhere a deal of slime, and this we traced all over the valley among the great toadstool plants; but, beyond that which I have already remarked, we found nothing. Nay, but I was near to forgetting, we found a quantity of this thin slime upon those fungi which filled the end of the little valley nearest to our encampment, and here also we discovered many of them fresh broken or uprooted, and there was the same mark of the beast upon them all, and now I remember the dull thuds that I had heard in the night, and made little doubt but that the creatures had climbed the great toadstools so that they might spy us out; and it may be that many climbed upon one, so that their weight broke the fungi, or uprooted them. At least, so the thought came to me.

And so we made an end of our search, and after that, the bo'sun set each one of us to work. But first he had us all back to the beach to give a hand to turn over the boat, so that he might get to the damaged part. Now, having the bottom of the boat full to his view, he made discovery that there was other damage beside that of the burst plank; for the bottom plank of all had come away from the keel, which seemed to us a very serious matter; though it did not show when the boat was upon her bilges. Yet the bo'sun assured us that he had no doubts but that she could be made seaworthy; though it would take a greater while than hitherto he had thought needful.

Having concluded his examination of the boat, the bo'sun sent one of the men to bring the bottom-boards out of the tent; for he needed some planking for the repair of the damage. Yet when the boards had been brought, he needed still something which they could not supply, and this was a length of very sound wood of some three inches in breadth each way, which he intended to bolt against the starboard side of the keel, after he had gotten the planking replaced so far as was possible. He had hopes that by means of this device he would be able to nail the bottom plank to this, and then caulk it with oakum, so making the boat almost so sound as ever.

Now hearing him express his need for such a piece of timber, we were all adrift to know from whence such a thing could be gotten, until there came suddenly to me a memory of the mast and topmast upon the other side of the island, and at once I made mention of them. At that, the bo'sun nodded, saying that we might get the timber out of it, though it would be a work requiring some considerable labour, in that we had only a hand-saw and a small hatchet. Then he sent us across to be getting it clear of the weed, promising to follow when he had made an end of trying to get the two displaced planks back into position.

Having reached the spars, we set-to with a very good will to shift away the weed and wrack that was piled over them, and very much entangled with the rigging. Presently we had laid them bare, and so we discovered them to be in remarkably sound condition, the lower-mast especially being a fine piece of timber. All the lower and topmast standing rigging was still attached, though in places the lower rigging was stranded so far as half-way up the shrouds; yet there remained much that was good and all of it quite free from rot, and of the very finest quality of white hemp, such as is to be seen only in the best found vessels.

About the time that we had finished clearing the weed, the bo'sun came over to us, bringing with him the saw and the hatchet. Under his directions, we cut the lanyards of the topmast rigging, and after that sawed through the topmast just above the cap. Now this was a very tough piece of work, and employed us a great part of the morning, even though we took turn and turn at the saw, and when it was done we were mightily glad that the bo'sun bade one of the men go over with some weed and make up the fire for dinner, after which he was to put on a piece of the salt meat to boil.

In the meanwhile, the bo'sun had started to cut through the topmast, about fifteen feet beyond the first cut, for that was the length of the batten he required; yet so wearisome was the work, that we had not gotten more than half through with it before the man whom the bo'sun had sent, returned to say that the dinner was ready. When this was dispatched, and we had rested a little over our pipes, the bo'sun rose and led us back; for he was determined to get through with the topmast before dark.

Presently, relieving each other frequently, we completed the second cut, and after that the bo'sun set us to saw a block about twelve inches deep from the remaining portion of the topmast. From this, when we had cut it, he proceeded to hew wedges with the hatchet. Then he notched the end of the fifteen-foot log, and into the notch he drove the wedges, and so, towards evening, as much, maybe, by good luck as good management, he had divided the log into two halves—the split running very fairly down the centre.

Now, perceiving how that it drew near to sundown, he bade the men haste and gather weed and carry it across to our camp; but one he sent along the shore to make a search for shell-fish among the weed; yet he himself ceased not to work at the divided log, and kept me with him as helper. Thus, within the next hour, we had a length, maybe some four inches in diameter, split off the whole length of one of the halves, and with this he was very well content; though it seemed but a very little result for so much labour.

By this time the dusk was upon us, and the men,

having made an end of weed carrying, were returned to us, and stood about, waiting for the bo'sun to go into camp. At this moment, the man the bo'sun had sent to gather shell-fish, returned, and he had a great crab upon his spear, which he had spitted through the belly. This creature could not have been less than a foot across the back, and had a very formidable appearance; yet it proved to be a most tasty matter for our supper, when it had been placed for a while in boiling water.

Now so soon as this man was returned, we made at once for the camp, carrying with us the piece of timber which we had hewn from the topmast. By this time it was quite dusk, and very strange amid the great fungi as we struck across the upper edge of the valley to the opposite beach. Particularly, I noticed that the hateful, mouldy odour of these monstrous vegetables was more offensive than I had found it to be in the day-time; though this may be because I used my nose the more, in that I could not use my eyes to any great extent.

We had gotten half way across the top of the valley, and the gloom was deepening steadily, when there stole to me upon the calmness of the evening air, a faint smell; something quite different from that of the surrounding fungi. A moment later I got a great whiff of it, and was near sickened with the abomination of it; but the memory of that foul thing which had come to the side of the boat in the dawn-gloom, before we discovered the island, roused me to a terror beyond that of the sickness of my stomach; for, suddenly, I knew what manner of thing it was that had beslimed my face and throat upon the previous night, and left its hideous stench lingering in my nostrils. And with the knowledge, I cried out to the bo'sun to make haste, for there were demons with us in the valley. And at that, some of the men made to run; but he bade them, in a very grim voice, stay where they were, and keep well together, else would they be attacked and over-come, straggled all among the fungi in the dark. And this, being, I doubt not, as much in fear of the rounding dark as of the bo'sun, they did, and so we came safely out of the valley; though there seemed to follow us a little lower down the slope an uncanny slithering.

Now, so soon as we reached the camp, the bo'sun ordered four fires to be lit—one on each side of the tent, and this we did, lighting them at the embers of our old fire, which we had most foolishly allowed to die down. When the fires had been got going, we put on the boiler, and treated the great crab as I have already mentioned, and so fell-to upon a very hearty supper; but, as we ate, each man had his weapon stuck in the sand beside him; for we had knowledge that the valley held some devilish thing, or maybe many; though the knowing did not spoil our appetites.

And so, presently, we came to an end of eating, whereat each man pulled out his pipe, intending to smoke; but the bo'sun told one of the men to get him upon his feet and keep watch, else might we be in danger of surprise, with every man lolling upon the sand; and this seemed to me very good sense; for it was easy to see that the men, too readily, deemed themselves secure, by reason of the brightness of the fires about them.

Now whilst the men were taking their ease within the circle of the fires, the bo'sun lit one of the dips which we had out of the ship in the creek, and went in to see how Job was, after the day's rest. At that, I rose up, reproaching myself for having forgotten the poor lad, and followed the bo'sun into the tent. Yet, I had but reached the opening, when he gave out a loud cry, and held the candle low down to the sand. At that, I saw the reason for his agitation; for, in the place where we had left Job, there was nothing. I stepped into the tent, and, in the same instant, there came to my nostrils the faint odour of the horrible stench which had come to me in the valley, and before then from the thing that came to the side of the boat. And, suddenly, I knew that Job had fallen prey of those foul things, and, knowing this, I called out to the bo'sun that *they* had taken the boy, and then my eyes caught the smear of slime upon the sand, and I had proof that I was not mistaken.

Now, so soon as the bo'sun knew all that was in my mind; though indeed it did but corroborate that which had come to his own, he came swiftly out from the tent, bidding the men to stand back; for they had come all about the entrance, being very much discomposed at that which the bo'sun had discovered. Then the bo'sun took from a faggot of the reeds, which they had cut at the time when he had bidden them gather fuel, several of the thickest, and to one of these he bound a great mass of the dry weed; whereupon the men, divining his intention, did likewise with the others, and so we had each of us the wherewithal for a mighty torch.

So soon as we had completed our preparations, we took each man his weapon and, plunging our torches into the fires, set off along the track which had been made by the devil-things and the body of poor Job; for now that we had suspicion that harm had come to him, the marks in the sand, and the slime, were very plain to be seen, so that it was wonderful that we had not discovered them earlier.

Now the bo'sun led the way, and, finding the marks led direct to the valley, he broke into a run, holding his torch well above his head. At that, each of us did likewise; for we had a great desire to be together, and further than this, I think with truth I may say, we were all fierce to avenge Job, so that we had less of fear in our hearts than otherwise had been the case.

In less than the half of a minute we had reached the end of the valley; but here, the ground being of a nature not happy in the revealing of tracks, we were

at fault to know in which direction to continue. At
that, the bo'sun set up a loud shout to Job, perchance
he might be yet alive; but there came no answer to us,
save a low and uncomfortable echo. Then the bo'sun,
desiring to waste no more time, ran straight down towards the centre of the valley, and we followed, and
kept our eyes very open about us. We had gotten perhaps half way, when one of the men shouted that he
saw something ahead; but the bo'sun had seen it earlier;
for he was running straight down upon it, holding his
torch high and swinging his great cutlass. Then, instead of smiting, he fell upon his knees beside it, and
the following instant we were up with him, and in that
same moment it seemed to me that I saw a number of
white shapes melt swiftly into the shadows further
ahead; but I had no thought for these when I perceived that by which the bo'sun knelt; for it was the
stark body of Job, and no inch of it but was covered
with the little ringed marks that I had discovered upon
my throat, and from every place there ran a trickle of
blood, so that he was a most horrid and fearsome sight.

At the sight of Job so mangled and be-bled, there
came over us the sudden quiet of a mortal terror, and
in that space of silence, the bo'sun placed his hand
over the poor lad's heart; but there was no movement,
though the body was still warm. Immediately upon
that, he rose to his feet, a look of vast wrath upon his
great face. He plucked his torch from the ground, into
which he had plunged the haft, and stared round into
the silence of the valley; but there was no living thing
in sight, nothing save the giant fungi and the strange
shadows cast by our great torches, and the loneliness.

At this moment, one of the men's torches, having
burnt near out, fell all to pieces, so that he held nothing
but the charred support, and immediately two more
came to a like end. Upon this, we became afraid that
they would not last us back to the camp, and we looked
to the bo'sun to know his wish; but the man was very

silent, and peering everywhere into the shadows. Then
a fourth torch fell to the ground in a shower of embers,
and I turned to look. In the same instant there came a
great flare of light behind me, accompanied by the dull
thud of a dry matter set suddenly alight. I glanced
swiftly back to the bo'sun, and he was staring up at
one of the giant toadstools which was in flames all
along its nearer edge, and burning with an incredible
fury, sending out spirits of flame, and anon giving out
sharp reports, and at each report a fine powder was
belched in thin streams; which, getting into our throats
and nostrils, set us sneezing and coughing most lamen-
tably; so that I am convinced, had any enemy come upon us at that moment, we had been undone by reason
of our uncouth helplessness.

Now whether it had come to the bo'sun to set alight
this first of the fungi, I know not; for it may be that
his torch coming by chance against it, set it afire. However it chanced, the bo'sun took it as a veritable hint
from Providence, and was already setting his torch to
one a little further off, whilst the rest of us were near to
choking with our coughings and sneezings. Yet, for all
that we were so suddenly overcome by the potency of
the powder, I doubt if a full minute passed before we
were each one busied after the manner of the bo'sun;
and those whose torches had burned out, knocked
flaming pieces from the burning fungus, and with
these impaled upon their torch-sticks, did so much execution as any.

And thus it happened that within five minutes of the
discovery of Job's body, the whole of that hideous
valley sent up to heaven the reek of its burning; whilst
we, filled with murderous desires, ran hither and thither
with our weapons, seeking to destroy the vile creatures
that had brought the poor lad to so unholy a death.
Yet nowhere could we discover any brute or creature
upon which to ease our vengeance, and so, presently,
the valley becoming impassable by reason of the heat,

the flying sparks and the abundance of the acrid dust, we made back to the body of the boy, and bore him thence to the shore.

And during all that night no man of us slept, and the burning of the fungi sent up a mighty pillar of flame out of the valley, as out of the mouth of a monstrous pit and when the morning came it still burned. Then when it was daylight, some of us slept, being greatly awearied; but some kept watch.

And when we waked there was a great wind and rain upon the island.

X: The Light in the Weed

Now the wind was very violent from the sea, and threatened to blow down our tent, the which, indeed, it achieved at last as we made an end of a cheerless breakfast. Yet, the bo'sun bade us not trouble to put it up again; but spread it out with the edges raised upon props made from the reeds, so that we might catch some of the rain water; for it was become imperative that we should renew our supply before putting out again to sea. And whilst some of us were busied about this, he took the others and set up a small tent made of the spare canvas, and under this he sheltered all of our matters like to be harmed by the rain.

In a little, the rain continuing very violent, we had near a breaker-full of water collected in the canvas, and were about to run it off into one of the breakers, when the bo'sun cried out to us to hold, and first taste the water before we mixed it with that which we had already. At that, we put down our hands and scooped up some of the water to taste, and thus we discovered it to be brackish and quite undrinkable, at which I was amazed, until the bo'sun reminded us that the canvas had been saturated for many days with salt water, so that it would take a great quantity of fresh before all the salt was washed out. Then he told us to lay it flat upon the beach, and scour it well on both sides with the sand, which we did, and afterwards let the rain rinse it well, whereupon the next water that we caught we found to be near fresh; though not sufficiently so for our purpose. Yet when we had rinsed it once more, it became clear of the salt, so that we were able to keep all that we caught further.

And then, something before noon, the rain ceased to fall, though coming again at odd times in short squalls; yet the wind died not, but blew steadily, and continued so from that quarter during the remainder of the time that we were upon the island.

Upon the ceasing of the rain, the bo'sun called us all together, that we might make a decent burial of the unfortunate lad, whose remains had lain during the night upon one of the bottom-boards of the boat. After a little discussion, it was decided to bury him in the beach; for the only part where there was soft earth was in the valley, and none of us had a stomach for that place. Moreover, the sand was soft and easy to dig, and as we had no proper tools, this was a great consideration. Presently, using the bottom-boards and the oars and the hatchet, we had a place large and deep enough to hold the boy, and into this we placed him. We made no prayer over him; but stood about the grave for a little space, in silence. Then, the bo'sun signed to us to fill in the sand; and, therewith, we covered up the poor lad, and left him to his sleep.

And, presently, we made our dinner; after which the bo'sun served out to each one of us a very sound tot of the rum; for he was minded to bring us back again to a cheerful state of mind.

After we had sat awhile, smoking, the bo'sun divided us into two parties to make a search through the island among the rocks, perchance we should find water, collected from the rain, among the hollows and crevasses; for though we had gotten some, through our device with the sail, yet we had by no means caught sufficient for our needs. He was especially anxious for haste, in that the sun had come out again; for he was feared that such small pools as we should find would be speedily dried up by its heat.

Now the bo'sun headed one party, and set the big seaman over the other, bidding all to keep their weapons very handy. Then he set out to the rocks about the base of the nearer hill, sending the others to the farther and greater one, and in each party we carried an empty breaker slung from a couple of the stout reeds, so that we might put all such driblets as we should find, straight away into it, before they had time to vanish into the hot air; and for the purpose of bailing up the water, we had brought with us our tin pannikins, and one of the boat's bailers.

In a while, and after much scrambling amid the rocks, we came upon a little pool of water that was remarkably sweet and fresh, and from this we removed near three gallons before it became dry; and after that we came across, maybe, five or six others; but not one of them near so big as the first; yet we were not displeased; for we had near three parts filled the breaker, and so we made back to the camp, having some wonder as to the luck of the other party.

When we came near the camp, we found the others returned before us, and seeming in a very high content with themselves; so that we had no need to call to them as to whether they had filled their breaker. When they saw us, they set out to us at a run to tell us that they had come upon a great basin of fresh water in a deep hollow a third of the distance up the side of the far hill, and at this the bo'sun bade us put down our breaker and make all of us to the hill, so that he might examine for himself whether their news was so good as it seemed.

Presently, being guided by the other party, we passed around to the back of the far hill, and discovered it to go upward to the top at an easy slope, with many ledges and broken places, so that it was scarce more difficult than a stair to climb. And so, having climbed perhaps ninety or a hundred feet, we came suddenly upon the place which held the water, and found that they had not made too much of their discovery; for the pool was near twenty feet long by twelve broad, and so clear as though it had come from a fountain; yet it had considerable depth, as we discovered by thrusting a spear shaft down into it.

Now the bo'sun, having seen for himself how good a supply of water there was for our needs, seemed very much relieved in his mind, and declared that within three days at the most we might leave the island, at which we felt none of us any regret. Indeed, had the boat escaped harm, we had been able to leave that same day; but this could not be; for there was much to be done before we had her seaworthy again.

Having waited until the bo'sun had made complete his examination, we turned to descend, thinking that this would be the bo'sun's intention; but he called to us to stay, and, looking back, we saw that he made to finish the ascent of the hill. At that, we hastened to follow him; though we had no notion of his reason for going higher. Presently, we were come to the top, and here we found a very spacious place, nicely level save that in one or two parts it was crossed by deepish cracks, maybe half a foot to a foot wide, and perhaps three to six fathoms long; but, apart from these and some great boulders, it was, as I have mentioned, a spacious place; moreover it was bone dry and pleasantly firm under one's feet, after so long upon the sand.

I think, even thus early, I had some notion of the bo'sun's design; for I went to the edge that overlooked the valley, and peered down, and, finding it nigh a sheer precipice, found myself nodding my head, as though it were in accordance with some part formed wish. Presently, looking about me, I discovered the

bo'sun to be surveying that part which looked over
towards the weed, and I made across to join him.
Here, again, I saw that the hill fell away very sheer,
and after that we went across to the seaward edge,
and there it was near as abrupt as on the weed side.

Then, having by this time thought a little upon the
matter, I put it straight to the bo'sun that here would
make indeed a very secure camping place, with nothing
to come at us upon our sides or back; and our front,
where was the slope, could be watched with ease. And
this I put to him with great warmth; for I was mortally
in dread of the coming night.

Now when I had made an end of speaking, the
bo'sun disclosed to me that this was, as I had sus-
picioned, his intent, and immediately he called to the
men that we should haste down, and ship our camp to
the top of the hill. At that, the men expressed their
approbation, and we made haste every one of us to the
camp, and began straightway to move our gear to the
hill-top.

In the meanwhile, the bo'sun, taking me to assist
him, set-to again upon the boat, being intent to get
his batten nicely shaped and fit to the side of the keel,
so that it would bed well to the keel, but more particularly to the plank which had sprung outward from
its place. And at this he laboured the greater part of
that afternoon, using the little hatchet to shape the
wood, which he did with surprising skill; yet when the
evening was come, he had not brought it to his liking.
But it must not be thought that he did naught but
work at the boat; for he had the men to direct, and
once he had to make his way to the top of the hill to
fix the place for the tent. And after the tent was up, he
set them to carry the dry weed to the new camp, and
at this he kept them until near dusk; for he had vowed
never again to be without a sufficiency of fuel. But two
of the men he sent to collect shell-fish—putting two
of them to the task, because he would not have one

alone upon the island, not knowing but that there might be danger, even though it were bright day; and a most happy ruling it proved; for, a little past the middle of the afternoon, we heard them shouting at the other end of the valley, and, not knowing but that they were in need of assistance, we ran with all haste to discover the reason of their calling, passing along the right-hand side of the blackened and sodden vale. Upon reaching the further beach, we saw a most incredible sight; for the two men were running towards us through the thick masses of the weed, while, no more than four or five fathoms behind, they were pursued by an enormous crab. Now I had thought the crab we had tried to capture before coming to the island, a prodigy unsurpassed; but this creature was more than treble its size, seeming as though a prodigious table were a-chase of them, and moreover, spite of its monstrous bulk, it made better way over the weed than I should have conceived to be possible—running almost sideways, and with one enormous claw raised near a dozen feet into the air.

Now whether, omitting accidents, the men would have made good their escape to the firmer ground of the valley, where they could have attained to a greater speed, I do not know; but suddenly one of them tripped over a loop of the weed, and the next instant lay helpless upon his face. He had been dead the following moment, but for the pluck of his companion, who faced round manfully upon the monster, and ran at it with his twenty-foot spear. It seemed to me that the spear took it about a foot below the overhanging armour of the great back shell, and I could see that it penetrated some distance into the creature, the man having, by the aid of Providence, stricken it in a vulnerable part. Upon receiving this thrust, the mighty crab ceased at once its pursuit, and clipped at the haft of the spear with its great mandible, snapping the weapon more easily than I had done the same thing to a straw. By the time we had raced up to the men, the one who had stumbled was again upon his feet, and turning to assist his comrade; but the bo'sun snatched his spear from him, and leapt forward himself; for the crab was making now at the other man. Now the bo'sun did not attempt to thrust the spear into the monster; but instead he made two swift blows at the great protruding eyes, and in a moment the creature had curled itself up, helpless, save that the huge claw waved about aimlessly. At that, the bo'sun drew us off, though the man who had attacked the crab desired to make an end of it, averring that we should get some very good eating out of it; but to this the bo'sun would not listen, telling him that it was yet capable of very deadly mischief, did any but come within reach of its prodigious mandible.

And after this, he bade them look no more for shell-fish; but take out the two fishing-lines which we had, and see if they could catch aught from some safe ledge on the further side of the hill upon which we had made our camp. Then he returned to his mending of the boat.

It was a little before the evening came down upon the island, that the bo'sun ceased work; and, after that, he called to the men, who, having made an end of their fuel carrying, were standing near, to place the full breakers—which we had not thought needful to carry to the new camp on account of their weight—under the upturned boat, some holding up the gunnel whilst the others pushed them under. Then the bo'sun laid the unfinished batten along with them, and we lowered the boat again over all, trusting to its weight to prevent any creature from meddling with aught.

After that, we made at once to the camp, being wearifully tired, and with a hearty anticipation of supper. Upon reaching the hilltop, the men whom the bo'sun had sent with the lines, came to show him a very fine fish, something like to a huge king-fish, which they had caught a few minutes earlier. This, the bo'sun, after examining, did not hesitate to pronounce fit for food; whereupon they set-to and opened and cleaned it. Now, as I have said, it was not unlike a great king-fish, and like it, had a mouth full of very formidable teeth; the use of which I understood the better when I saw the contents of its stomach, which seemed to consist of nothing but the coiled tentacles of squid or cuttle-fish, with which, as I have shown, the weed-continent swarmed. When these were upset upon the rock, I was confounded to perceive the length and thickness of some of them; and could only conceive that this particular fish must be a very desperate enemy to them, and able successfully to attack monsters of a bulk infinitely greater than its own.

After this, and whilst the supper was preparing, the bo'sun called to some of the men to put up a piece of the spare canvas upon a couple of the reeds, so as to make a screen against the wind, which up there was so fresh that it came near at times to scattering the fire abroad. This they found not difficult; for a little on the windward side of the fire there ran one of the cracks of which I have made previous mention, and into this they jammed the supports, and so in a very little time had the fire screened.

Presently, the supper was ready, and I found the fish to be very fair eating; though somewhat coarse; but this was no great matter for concern with so empty a stomach as I contained. And here I would remark, that we made our fishing save our provisions through all our stay on the island. Then, after we had come to an end of our eating, we lay down to a most comfortable smoke; for we had no fear of attack, at that height, and with precipices upon all sides save that which lay in front. Yet, so soon as we had rested and smoked a while, the bo'sun set the watches; for he would run no risk through carelessness.

By this time the night was drawing on apace; yet it

was not so dark but that one could perceive matters at a very reasonable distance. Presently, being in a mood that tended to thoughtfulness, and feeling a desire to be alone for a little, I strolled away from the fire to the leeward edge of the hill-top. Here, I paced up and down awhile, smoking and meditating. Anon, I would stare out across the immensity of the vast continent of weed and slime that stretched its incredible desolation out beyond the darkening horizon, and there would come the thought to me of the terror of men whose vessels had been entangled among its strange growths, and so my thoughts came to the lone derelict that lay out there in the dusk, and I fell to wondering what had been the end of her people, and at that I grew yet more solemn in my heart. For it seemed to me that they must have died at last by starvation, and if not by that, then by the act of some one of the devil-creatures which inhabited that lonely weed-world. And then, even as I fell upon this thought, the bo'sun clapt me upon the shoulder, and told me in a very hearty way to come to the light of the fire, and banish all melancholy thoughts; for he had a very penetrating discernment, and had followed me quietly from the camping place, having had reason once or twice before to chide me for gloomy meditations. And for this, and many other matters, I had grown to like the man, the which I could almost believe at times, was his regarding of me; but his words were too few for me to gather his feelings; though I had hope that they were as I surmised.

And so I came back to the fire, and presently, it not being my time to watch until after midnight, I turned into the tent for a spell of sleep, having first arranged a comfortable spread of some of the softer portions of the dry weed to make me a bed.

Now I was very full of sleep, so that I slept heavily, and in this wise heard not the man on watch call the bo'sun; yet the rousing of the others waked me, and so

I came to myself and found the tent empty, at which I
ran very hurriedly to the doorway, and so discovered
that there was a clear moon in the sky, the which, by
reason of the cloudiness that had prevailed, we had
been without for the past two nights. Moreover, the
sultriness had gone, the wind having blown it away
with the clouds; yet though, maybe, I appreciated this,
it was but in a half-conscious manner; for I was put
about to discover the whereabouts of the men, and the
reason of their leaving the tent. With this purpose, I
stepped out from the entrance, and the following instant discovered them all in a clump beside the leeward
edge of the hill-top. At that, I held my tongue; for I
knew not but that silence might be their desire; but I
ran hastily over to them, and inquired of the bo'sun
what manner of thing it was which called them from
their sleep, and he, for answer, pointed out into the
greatness of the weed-continent.

At that, I stared out over the breadth of the weed,
showing very ghostly in the moonlight; but, for the
moment, I saw not the thing to which he purposed to
draw my attention. Then, suddenly, it fell within the
circle of my gaze—a little light out in the lonesomeness.
For the space of some moments, I stared with bewildered eyes; then it came to me with abruptness that
the light shone from the lone derelict lying out in the
weed, the same that, upon that very evening, I had
looked with sorrow and awe, because of the end of
those who had been in her—and now, behold, a light
burning, seemingly within one of her after cabins;
though the moon was scarce powerful enough to enable
the outline of the hulk to be seen clear of the rounding
wilderness.

And from this time, until the day, we had no more
sleep; but made up the fire, and sat round it, full of
excitement and wonder, and getting up continually to
discover if the light still burned. This it ceased to do

about an hour after I had first seen it; but it was the more proof that some of our kind were no more than the half of a mile from our camp.

And at last the day came.

XI: The Signals from the Ship

NOW SO SOON AS IT WAS CLEARLY LIGHT, WE WENT
all of us to the leeward brow of the hill to stare upon the
derelict, which now we had cause to believe no derelict, but an inhabited vessel. Yet though we watched
her for upwards of two hours, we could discover no
sign of any living creature, the which, indeed, had we
been in cooler minds, we had not thought strange, seeing that she was all so shut in by the great superstructure; but we were hot to see a fellow creature,
after so much lonesomeness and terror in strange lands
and seas, and so could not by any means contain ourselves in patience until those aboard the hulk should
choose to discover themselves to us.

And so, at last, being wearied with watching, we
made it up together to shout when the bo'sun should
give us the signal, by this means making a good volume of sound which we conceived the wind might carry
down to the vessel. Yet though we raised many shouts,
making as it seemed to us a very great noise, there
came no response from the ship, and at last we were
fain to cease from our calling, and ponder some other
way of bringing ourselves to the notice of those within
the hulk.

For awhile we talked, some proposing one thing, and

some another; but none of them seeming like to achieve our purpose. And after that we fell to marvelling that the fire which we had lit in the valley had not awakened them to the fact that some of their fellow creatures were upon the island; for, had it, we could not suppose but that they would have kept a perpetual watch upon the island until such time as they should have been able to attract our notice. Nay! more than this, it was scarce credible that they should not have made an answering fire, or set some of their bunting above the superstructure, so that our gaze should be arrested upon the instant we chanced to glance towards the hulk. But so far from this, there appeared even a purpose to shun our attention; for that light which we had viewed in the past night was more in the way of an accident, than of the nature of a purposeful exhibition.

And so, presently, we went to breakfast, eating heart-ily; our night of wakefulness having given us mighty appetites; but, for all that, we were so engrossed by the mystery of the lonesome craft, that I doubt if any of us knew what manner of food it was with which we filled our bellies. For first one view of the matter would be raised, and when this had been combated, another would be broached, and in this wise it came up finally that some of the men were falling in doubt whether the ship was inhabited by anything human, saying rather that it might be held by some demoniac creature of the great weed-continent. At this proposi-tion, there came among us a very uncomfortable silence; for not only did it chill the warmth of our hopes; but seemed like to provide us with a fresh terror, who were already acquainted with too much. Then the bo'sun spoke, laughing with a hearty contempt at our sudden fears, and pointed out that it was just as like that they aboard the ship had been put in fear by the great blaze from the valley, as that they should take it for a sign that fellow creatures and friends were at hand. For, as he put it to us, who of us could say what fell brutes and demons the weed-continent did hold, and if we had reason to know that there were very dread things among the weed, how much the more must they, who had, for all that we knew, been many years beset around by such. And so, as he went on to make clear, we might suppose that they were very well aware there had come some creatures to the island; yet, maybe, they desired not to make themselves known until they had been given sight of them, and because of this, we must wait until they chose to discover themselves to us.

Now when the bo'sun had made an end, we felt each one of us greatly cheered; for his discourse seemed very reasonable. Yet still there were many matters that troubled our company; for, as one put it, was it not mightily strange that we had not had previous sight of their light, or, in the day, of the smoke from their galley fire? But to this the bo'sun replied that our camp hitherto had lain in a place where we had not sight, even of the great world of weed, leaving alone any view of the derelict. And more, that at such times as we had crossed to the opposite beach, we had been occupied too sincerely to have much thought to watch the hulk, which, indeed, from that position showed only her great superstructure. Further, that, until the preceding day, we had but once climbed to any height; and that from our present camp the derelict could not be viewed, and to do so, we had to go near to the leeward edge of the hill-top.

And so, breakfast being ended, we went all of us to see if there were yet any signs of life in the hulk; but when an hour had gone, we were no wiser. Therefore, it being folly to waste further time, the bo'sun left one man to watch from the brow of the hill, charging him very strictly to keep in such position that he could be seen by any aboard the silent craft, and so took the rest down to assist him in the repairing of the boat. And from thence on, during the day, he gave the men a turn each at watching, telling them to wave to him should there come any sign from the hulk. Yet, excepting the watch, he kept every man so busy as might be, some bringing weed to keep up a fire which he had lit near the boat; one to help him turn and hold the batten upon which he laboured; and two he sent across to the wreck of the mast, to detach one of the futtock shrouds, which (as is most rare) were made of iron rods. This, when they brought it, he bade me heat in the fire, and afterwards beat out straight at one end, and when this was done, he set me to burn holes with it through the keel of the boat, at such places as he had marked, these being for the bolts with which he had determined to fasten on the batten.

In the meanwhile, he continued to shape the batten until it was a very good and true fit according to his liking. And all the while he cried out to this man and to that one to do this or that; and so I perceived that, apart from the necessity of getting the boat into a seaworthy condition, he was desirous to keep the men busied; for they were become so excited at the thought of fellow creatures almost within hail, that he could not hope to keep them sufficiently in hand without some matter upon which to employ them.

Now, it must not be supposed that the bo'sun had no share of our excitement; for I noticed that he gave ever and anon a glance to the crown of the far hill, perchance the watchman had some news for us. Yet the morning went by, and no signal came to tell us that the people in the ship had design to show themselves to the man upon watch, and so we came to dinner. At this meal, as might be supposed, we had a second discussion upon the strangeness of the behaviour of those aboard the hulk; yet none could give any more reasonable explanation than the bo'sun had given in the morning, and so we left it at that.

Presently, when we had smoked and rested very comfortably, for the bo'sun was no tyrant, we rose at his

bidding to descend once more to the beach. But at this
moment, one of the men having run to the edge of the
hill to take a short look at the hulk, cried out that a part
of the great superstructure over the quarter had been
removed, or pushed back, and that there was a figure
there, seeming, so far as his unaided sight could tell,
to be looking through a spy-glass at the island. Now it
would be difficult to tell of all our excitement at this
news, and we ran eagerly to see for ourselves if it could
be as he informed us. And so it was; for we could see
the person very clearly; though remote and small
because of the distance. That he had seen us, we discovered in a moment; for he began suddenly to wave
something, which I judged to be the spy-glass, in a
very wild manner, seeming also to be jumping up and
down. Yet, I doubt not but that we were as much excited; for suddenly I discovered myself to be shouting
with the rest in a most insane fashion, and moreover I
was waving my hands and running to and fro upon the
brow of the hill. Then, I observed that the figure on the
hulk had disappeared; but it was for no more than a
moment, and then it was back and there were near
a dozen with it, and it seemed to me that some of them
were females; but the distance was over great for surety.
Now these, all of them, seeing us upon the brow of the
hill, where we must have shown up plain against the
sky, began at once to wave in a very frantic way, and
we, replying in like manner, shouted ourselves hoarse
with vain greetings. But soon we grew wearied of the
unsatisfactoriness of this method of showing our excitement, and one took a piece of the square canvas, and
let it stream out into the wind, waving it to them, and
another took a second piece and did likewise, while a
third man rolled up a short bit into a cone and made
use of it as a speaking trumpet; though I doubt if his
voice carried any the further because of it. For my
part, I had seized one of the long bamboo-like reeds

which were lying about near the fire, and with this I
was making a very brave show. And so it may be seen
how very great and genuine was our exaltation upon
our discovery of these poor people shut off from the
world within that lonesome craft.

Then, suddenly, it seemed to come to us to realize
that *they* were among the weed, and *we* upon the hill-
top, and that we had no means of bridging that which
lay between. And at this we faced one another to
discuss what we should do to effect the rescue of those
within the hulk. Yet it was little that we could even
suggest; for though one spoke of how he had seen a
rope cast by means of a mortar to a ship that lay off
shore, yet this helped us not, for we had no mortar;
but here the same man cried out that they in the ship
might have such a thing, so that they would be able
to shoot the rope to us, and at this we thought more upon his saying; for if they had such a weapon, then
might our difficulties be solved. Yet we were greatly at
a loss to know how we should discover whether they
were possessed of one, and further to explain our design to them. But here the bo'sun came to our help, and
bade one man go quickly and char some of the reeds
in the fire, and whilst this was doing he spread out upon
the rock one of the spare lengths of canvas; then he
sung out to the man to bring him one of the pieces of
charred reed, and with this he wrote our question upon
the canvas, calling for fresh charcoal as he required it.
Then, having made an end of writing, he bade two of
the men take hold of the canvas by the ends, and expose
it to the view of those in the ship, and in this manner
we got them to understand our desires. For, presently,
some of them went away, and came back after a little,
and held up for us to see, a very great square of white,
and upon it a great "NO," and at this were we again
at our wits' ends to know how it would be possible to
rescue those within the ship; for, suddenly, our whole

desire to leave the island, was changed into a determination to rescue the people in the hulk, and, indeed, had our intentions not been such we had been veritable curs; though I am happy to tell that we had no thought at this juncture but for those who were now looking to us to restore them once more to the world to which they had been so long strangers.

Now, as I have said, we were again at our wits' ends to know how to come at those within the hulk, and there we stood all of us, talking together, perchance we should hit upon some plan, and anon we would turn and wave to those who watched us so anxiously. Yet, a while passed, and we had come no nearer to a method of rescue. Then a thought came to me (waked perchance by the mention of shooting the rope over to the hulk by means of a mortar) how that I had read once in a book, of a fair maid whose lover effected her escape from a castle by a similar artifice, only that in his case he made use of a bow in place of a mortar, and a cord instead of a rope, his sweetheart hauling up the rope by means of the cord.

Now it seemed to me a possible thing to substitute a bow for the mortar, if only we could find the material with which to make such a weapon, and with this in view, I took up one of the lengths of the bamboo-like reed, and tried the spring of it, which I found to be very good; for this curious growth, of which I have spoken hitherto as a reed, had no resemblance to that plant, beyond its appearance; it being extraordinarily tough and woody, and having considerably more nature than a bamboo. Now, having tried the spring of it, I went over to the tent and cut a piece of sampson-line which I found among the gear, and with this and the reed I contrived a rough bow. Then I looked about until I came upon a very young and slender reed which had been cut with the rest, and from this I fashioned some sort of an arrow, feathering it with a piece of one of the broad, stiff leaves, which grew upon the plant, and after that I went forth to the crowd about the leeward edge of the hill. Now when they saw me thus armed, they seemed to think that I intended a jest, and some of them laughed, conceiving that it was a very odd action on my part; but when I explained that which was in my mind, they ceased from laughter, and shook their heads, making that I did but waste time; for, as they said, nothing save gunpowder could cover so great a distance. And after that they turned again to the bo'sun with whom some of them seemed to be in argument. And so for a little space I held my peace, and listened; thus I discovered that certain of the men advocated the taking of the boat—so soon as it was sufficiently repaired—and making a passage through the weed to the ship, which they proposed to do by cutting a narrow canal. But the bo'sun shook his head, and reminded them of the great devil-fish and crabs, and the worse things which the weed concealed, saying that those in the ship would have done it long since had it been possible, and at that the men were silenced, being robbed of their unreasoning ardour by his warnings.

Now just at this point there happened a thing which proved the wisdom of that which the bo'sun contended; for, suddenly, one of the men cried out to us to look, and at that we turned quickly, and saw that there was a great commotion among those who were in the open place in the superstructure; for they were running this way and that, and some were pushing to the slide which filled the opening. And then, immediately, we saw the reason for their agitation and haste; for there was a stir in the weed near to the stern of the ship, and the next instant, monstrous tentacles were reached up to the place where had been the opening; but the door was shut, and those aboard the hulk in safety. At this manifestation, the men about me who had proposed to make use of the boat, and the others also, cried out their horror of the vast creature, and, I am convinced, had the rescue depended upon their use of the boat, then had those in the hulk been forever doomed.

Now, conceiving that this was a good point at which to renew my importunities, I began once again to explain the probabilities of my plan succeeding, addressing myself more particularly to the bo'sun. I told how that I had read that the ancients made mighty weapons, some of which could throw a great stone so heavy as two men, over a distance surpassing a quarter of a mile; moreover, that they compassed huge catapults which threw a lance, or great arrow, even further. On this, he expressed much surprise, never having heard of the like; but doubted greatly that we should be able to construct such a weapon. Yet, I told him that I was prepared; for I had the plan of one clearly in my mind, and further I pointed out to him that we had the wind in our favour, and that we were a great height up, which would allow the arrow to travel the farther before it came so low as the weed.

Then I stepped to the edge of the hill, and, bidding him watch, fitted my arrow to the string, and, having bent the bow, loosed it, whereupon, being aided by the wind and the height on which I stood, the arrow plunged into the weed at a distance of near two hundred yards from where we stood, that being about a quarter of the distance on the road to the derelict. At that, the bo'sun was won over to my idea; though, as he remarked, the arrow had fallen nearer had it been drawing a length of yarn after it, and to this I assented; but pointed out that my bow-and-arrow was but a rough affair, and, more, that I was no archer; yet I promised him, with the bow that I should make, to cast a shaft clean over the hulk, did he but give me his assistance, and bid the men to help.

Now, as I have come to regard it in the light of

greater knowledge, my promise was exceeding rash; but I had faith in my conception, and was very eager to put it to the test; the which, after much discussion at supper, it was decided I should be allowed to do.

XII: The Making of the Great Bow

THE FOURTH NIGHT UPON THE ISLAND WAS THE FIRST to pass without incident. It is true that a light showed from the hulk out in the weed; but now that we had made some acquaintance with her inmates, it was no longer a cause for excitement, so much as contemplation. As for the valley where the vile things had made an end of Job, it was very silent and desolate under the moonlight; for I made a point to go and view it during my time on watch; yet, for all that it lay empty, it was very dree, and a place to conjure up uncomfortable thoughts, so that I spent no great time pondering it.

This was the second night on which we had been free from the terror of the devil-things, and it seemed to me that the great fire had put them in fear of us and driven them away; but of the truth or error of this idea, I was to learn later.

Now it must be admitted that, apart from a short look into the valley, and occasional starings at the light out in the weed, I gave little attention to aught but my plans for the great bow, and to such use did I put my time, that when I was relieved, I had each particular and detail worked out, so that I knew very well just what to set the men doing so soon as we should make a start in the morning.

Presently, when the morning had come, and we had made an end of breakfast, we turned-to upon the great bow, the bo'sun directing the men under my supervision. Now, the first matter to which I bent attention, was the raising, to the top of the hill, of the remaining half of that portion of the topmast which the bo'sun had split in twain to procure the batten for the boat. To this end, we went down, all of us, to the beach where lay the wreckage, and, getting about the portion which I intended to use, carried it to the foot of the hill; then we sent a man to the top to let down the rope by which we had moored the boat to the sea anchor, and when we had bent this on securely to the piece of timber, we returned to the hill-top, and tailed on to the rope, and so, presently, after much weariful pulling, had it up.

The next thing I desired was that the split face of the timber should be dubbed straight, and this the bo'sun understood to do, and whilst he was about it, I went with some of the men to the grove of reeds, and here, with great care, I made a selection of some of the finest, these being for the bow, and after that I cut some which were very clean and straight, intending them for the great arrows. With these we returned once more to the camp, and there I set-to and trimmed them of their leaves, keeping these latter, for I had a use for them. The I took a dozen reeds and cut them each to a length of twenty-five feet, and afterwards notched them for the strings. In the meanwhile, I had sent two men down to the wreckage of the masts to cut away a couple of the hempen shrouds and bring them to the camp, and they, appearing about this time, I set to work to unlay the shrouds, so that they might get out the fine white yarns which lay beneath the outer covering of tar and blacking. These, when they had come at them, we found to be very good and sound, and this being so, I bid them make three-yarn sennit; meaning it for the strings of the bows. Now, it will be observed that I have said bow*s*, and this I will explain. It had been my original intention to make one great bow, lashing a dozen of the reeds together for the purpose; but this, upon pondering it, I conceived to be but a poor plan; for there would be much life and power lost in the rendering of each piece through the lashings, when the bow was released. To obviate this, and further, to compass the bending of the bow, the which had, at first, been a source of puzzlement to me as to how it was to be accomplished, I had determined to make twelve separate bows, and these I intended to fasten at the end of the stock one above the other, so that they were all in one plane vertically, and because of this conception, I should be able to bend the bows one at a time, and slip each string over the catch-notch, and afterwards frap the twelve strings together in the middle part so that they would be but one string to the butt of the arrow. All this, I explained to the bo'sun, who, indeed, had been exercised in his own mind as to how we should be able to bend such a bow as I intended to make, and he was mightily pleased with my method of evading this difficulty, and also one other, which, else, had been greater than the bending, and that was the *stringing* of the bow, which would have proved a very awkward work.

Presently, the bo'sun called out to me that he had got the surface of the stock sufficiently smooth and nice; and at that I went over to him; for now I wished him to burn a slight groove down the centre, running from end to end, and this I desired to be done very exactly; for upon it depended much of the true flight of the arrow. Then I went back to my own work; for I had not yet finished notching the bows. Presently, when I had made an end of this, I called for a length of the sennit, and, with the aid of another man, contrived to string one of the bows. This, when I had finished, I found to be very springy, and so stiff to bend that I had all that I could manage to do so, and at this I felt very satisfied.

Presently, it occurred to me that I should do well to set some of the men to work upon the line which the arrow was to carry; for I had determined that this should be made also from the white hemp yarns, and, for the sake of lightness, I conceived that one thickness of yarn would be sufficient; but so that it might compass enough of strength, I bid them split the yarns and lay the two halves up together, and in this manner they made me a very light and sound line; though it must not be supposed that it was finished at once; for I needed over half a mile of it, and thus it was later finished than the bow itself.

Having now gotten all things in train, I set me down to work upon one of the arrows; for I was anxious to see what sort of a fist I should make of them, knowing how much would depend upon the balance and truth of the missile. In the end, I made a very fair one, feathering it with its own leaves, and trueing and smoothing it with my knife; after which I inserted a small bolt in the forrard end, to act as a head, and, as I conceived, give it balance; though whether I was right in this latter, I am unable to say. Yet, before I had finished my arrow, the bo'sun had made the groove, and called me over to him, that I might admire it, the which I did; for it was done with a wonderful neatness.

Now I have been so busy with my description of how we made the great bow, that I have omitted to tell of the flight of time, and how we had eaten our dinner this long while since, and how that the people in the hulk had waved to us, and we had returned their signals, and then written upon a length of the canvas the one word, "WAIT". And, besides all this, some had gathered our fuel for the coming night.

And so, presently, the evening came upon us; but we ceased not to work; for the bo'sun bade the men to light a second great fire, beside our former one, and by the light of this we worked another long spell; though it seemed short enough, by reason of the interest of the work. Yet, at last, the bo'sun bade us to stop and make supper, which we did, and after that, he sat the watches, and the rest of us turned in; for we were very weary.

In spite of my previous weariness, when the man whom I relieved called me to take my watch, I felt very fresh and wide awake, and spent a great part of the time, as on the preceding night, in studying over my plans for completing the great bow, and it was then that I decided finally in what manner I would secure the bows athwart the end of the stock; for until then I had been in some little doubt, being divided between several methods. Now, however, I concluded to make twelve grooves across the sawn end of the stock, and fit the middles of the bows into these, one above the other, as I have already mentioned; and then to lash them at each side to bolts driven into the sides of the stock. And with this idea I was very well pleased; for it promised to make them secure, and this without any great amount of work.

Now, though I spent much of my watch in thinking over the details of my prodigious weapon, yet it must not be supposed that I neglected to perform my duty as watchman; for I walked continually about the top of the hill, keeping my cut-and-thrust ready for any sudden emergency. Yet my time passed off quietly enough; though it is true that I witnessed one thing which brought me a short spell of disquiet thought. It was in this wise:—I had come to that part of the hill-top which overhung the valley, and it came to me, abruptly, to go near to the edge and look over. Thus, the moon being very bright, and the desolation of the valley reasonably clear to the eye, it appeared to me, as I looked that I saw a movement among certain of the fungi which had not burnt, but stood up shrivelled and blackened in the valley. Yet by no means could I be sure that it was not a sudden fancy, born of the eeriness of that desolate-looking vale; the more so as I was like to be deceived because of the uncertainty which the light of the moon gives. Yet, to prove my doubts, I went back until I had found a piece of rock easy to throw, and this, taking a short run, I cast into the valley, aiming at the spot where it had seemed to me that there had been a movement. Immediately upon this, I caught a glimpse of some moving thing, and then, more to my right, something else stirred, and at this, I looked towards it; but could discover nothing. Then, looking back at the clump at which I had aimed my missile, I saw that the slime-covered pool, which lay near, was all a-quiver, or so it seemed. Yet the next instant I was just as full of doubt; for, even as I watched it, I perceived that it was quite still. And after that, for some time, I kept a very strict gaze into the valley; yet could nowhere discover aught to prove my suspicions, and, at last, I ceased from watching it; for I feared to grow fanciful, and so wandered to that part of the hill which overlooked the weed.

Presently, when I had been relieved, I returned to sleep, and so till the morning. Then, when we had made each of us a hasty breakfast—for all were grown mightily keen to see the great bow completed—we set-to upon it, each at our appointed task. Thus, the bo'sun and I made it our work to make the twelve grooves athwart the flat end of the stock, into which I proposed to fit and lash the bows, and this we accomplished by means of the iron futtock-shroud, which we heated in its middle part, and then, each taking an end (protecting our hands with canvas), we went one on each side and applied the iron until at length we had the grooves burnt out very nicely and accurately. This work occupied us all the morning; for the grooves had to be deeply burnt; and in the meantime the men had completed near enough sennit for the stringing of the bows;

yet those who were at work on the line which the arrow was to carry, had scarce made more than half, so that I called off one man from the sennit to turn-to and give them a hand with the making of the line.

When dinner was ended, the bo'sun and I set-to about fitting the bows into their places, which we did, and lashed them to twenty-four bolts, twelve a side, driven into the timber of the stock, about twelve inches in from the end. After this, we bent and strung the bows, taking very great care to have each bent exactly as the one below it; for we started at the bottom. And so, before sunset, we had that part of our work ended.

Now, because the two fires which we had lit on the previous night had exhausted our fuel, the bo'sun deemed it prudent to cease work, and go down all of us to bring up a fresh supply of the dry seaweed and some faggots of the reeds. This we did, making an end of our journeyings just as the dusk came over the island. Then, having made a second fire, as on the preceding night, we had first our supper, and after that another spell of work, all the men turning to upon the line which the arrow was to carry, whilst the bo'sun and I set-to, each of us, upon the making of a fresh arrow; for I had realized that we should have to make one or two flights before we could hope to find our range and make true our aim.

Later, maybe about nine of the night, the bo'sun bade us all to put away our work, and then he set the watches, after which the rest of us went into the tent to sleep; for the strength of the wind made the shelter a very pleasant thing.

That night, when it came my turn to watch, I minded me to take a look into the valley; but though I watched at intervals through the half of an hour, I saw nothing to lead me to imagine that I had indeed seen aught on the previous night, and so I felt more confident in my mind that we should be troubled no further by the devil-things which had destroyed poor Job. Yet I must record one thing which I saw during my watch; though this was from the edge of the hill-top which overlooked the weed-continent, and was not in the valley, but in the stretch of clear water which lay between the island and the weed. As I saw it, it seemed to me that a number of great fish were swimming across from the island, diagonally towards the great continent of weed: they were swimming in one wake, and keeping a very regular line; but not breaking the water after the manner of porpoises or black fish. Yet, though I have mentioned this, it must not be supposed that I saw any very strange thing in such a sight, and indeed, I thought nothing more of it than to wonder what sort of fish they might be; for, as I saw them indistinctly in the moonlight, they made a queer appearance, seeming each of them to be possessed of two tails, and further, I could have thought I perceived a flicker as of tentacles just beneath the surface; but of this I was by no means sure.

Upon the following morning, having hurried our breakfast, each of us set-to again upon our tasks; for we were in hopes to have the great bow at work before dinner. Soon, the bo'sun had finished his arrow, and mine was completed very shortly after, so that there lacked nothing now to the completion of our work, save the finishing of the line, and the getting of the bow into position. This latter, assisted by the men, we proceeded now to effect, making a level bed of rocks near the edge of the hill which overlooked the weed. Upon this we placed the great bow, and then, having sent the men back to their work at the line, we proceeded to the aiming of the huge weapon. Now, when we had gotten the instrument pointed, as we conceived, straight over the hulk, the which we accomplished by squinting along the groove which the bo'sun had burnt down the centre of the stock, we turned-to upon the arranging of the notch and trigger, the notch being to hold the strings when the weapon was set, and the trigger—a board bolted on loosely at the side just below the notch—to push them upwards out of this place when we desired to discharge the bow. This part of the work took up no great portion of our time, and soon we had all ready for our first flight. Then we commenced to set the bows, bending the bottom one first, and then those above in turn, until all were set; and, after that, we laid the arrow very carefully in the groove. Then I took two pieces of spunyarn and frapped the strings together at each end of the notch, and by this means I was assured that all the strings would act in unison when striking the butt of the arrow. And so we had all things ready for the discharge; whereupon, I placed my foot upon the trigger, and, bidding the bo'sun watch carefully the flight of the arrow, pushed downwards. The next instant, with a mighty twang, and a quiver that made the great stock stir on its bed of rocks, the bow sprang to its lesser tension, hurling the arrow outwards and upwards in a vast arc. Now, it may be conceived with what mortal interest we watched its flight, and so in a minute discovered that we had aimed too much to the right; for the arrow struck the weed ahead of the hulk—but *beyond* it. At that, I was filled near to bursting with pride and joy, and the men who had come forward to witness the trial, shouted to acclaim my success, whilst the bo'sun clapt me twice upon the shoulder to signify his regard, and shouted as loud as any.

And now it seemed to me that we had but to get the true aim, and the rescue of those in the hulk would be but a matter of another day or two; for, having once gotten a line to the hulk, we should haul across a thin rope by its means, and with this a thicker one; after which we should set this up so taut as possible, and then bring the people in the hulk to the island by means of a seat and block which we should haul to and fro along the supporting line.

Now, having realized that the bow would indeed carry so far as the wreck, we made haste to try our second arrow, and at the same time we bade the men go back to their work upon the line; for we should have need of it in a very little while. Presently, having pointed the bow more to the left, I took the frappings off the strings, so that we could bend the bows singly, and after that we set the great weapon again. Then, seeing that the arrow was straight in the groove, I replaced the frappings, and immediately discharged it. This time, to my very great pleasure and pride, the arrow went with a wonderful straightness towards the ship, and, clearing the superstructure, passed out of our sight as it fell behind it. At this, I was all impatience to try to get the line to the hulk before we made our dinner; but the men had not yet laid-up sufficient; there being then only four hundred and fifty fathoms (which the bo'sun measured off by stretching it along his arms and across his chest). This being so, we went to dinner, and made very great haste through it; and, after that, every one of us worked at the line, and so in about an hour we had sufficient; for I had estimated that it would not be wise to make the attempt with a less length than five hundred fathoms.

Having now completed a sufficiency of the line, the bo'sun set one of the men to flake it down very carefully upon the rock beside the bow, whilst he himself tested it at all such parts as he thought in any way doubtful, and so, presently, all was ready. Then I bent it on to the arrow, and, having set the bow whilst the men were flaking down the line, I was prepared immediately to discharge the weapon.

Now, all the morning, a man upon the hulk had observed us through a spy-glass, from a position that brought his head just above the edge of the superstructure, and, being aware of our intentions—having watched the previous flights—he understood the bo'sun, when he beckoned to him, that we had made ready for a third shot, and so, with an answering wave of his spy-glass, he disappeared from our sight. At that, having first turned to see that all were clear of the line, I pressed down the trigger, my heart beating very fast and thick, and so in a moment the arrow was sped. But now, doubtless because of the weight of the line, it made nowhere near so good a flight as on the previous occasion, the arrow striking the weed some two hundred yards short of the hulk, and at this, I could near have wept with vexation and disappointment.

Immediately upon the failure of my shot, the bo'sun called to the men to haul in the line very carefully, so that it should not be parted through the arrow catching in the weed; then he came over to me, and proposed that we should set-to at once to make a heavier arrow, suggesting that it had been lack of weight in the missile which had caused it to fall short. At that, I felt once more hopeful, and turned-to at once to prepare a new arrow; the bo'sun doing likewise; though in his case he intended to make a lighter one than that which had failed; for, as he put it, though the heavier one fell short, yet might the lighter succeed, and if neither, then we could only suppose that the bow lacked power to carry the line, and in that case we should have to try some other method.

Now, in about two hours, I had made my arrow, the bo'sun having finished his a little earlier; and so (the men having hauled in all the line and flaked it down ready) we prepared to make another attempt to cast it over the hulk. Yet, a second time we failed, and by so much that it seemed hopeless to think of success; but, for all that it appeared useless, the bo'sun insisted on making a last try with the light arrow, and, presently, when we had gotten the line ready again, we loosed upon the wreck; but in this case so lamentable was our failure, that I cried out to the bo'sun to set the useless thing upon the fire and burn it; for I was sorely irked by its failure, and could scarce abide to speak civilly of it.

Now the bo'sun, perceiving how I felt, sung out that we would cease troubling about the hulk for the present, and go down all of us to gather reeds and weed for the fire; for it was drawing nigh to evening. And this we did, though all in a disconsolate condition of mind; for we had seemed so near to success, and now it appeared to be further than ever from us. And so, in a while, having brought up a sufficiency of fuel, the bo'sun sent two of the men down to one of the ledges which overhung the sea, and bade them see whether they could not secure a fish for our supper. Then, taking our places about the fire, we fell-to upon a discussion as to how we should come at the people in the hulk.

Now, for a while there came no suggestion worthy of notice, until at last there occurred to me a notable idea, and I called out suddenly that we should make a small fire balloon, and float off the line to them by such means. At that, the men about the fire were silent a moment; for the idea was new to them, and moreover they needed to comprehend just what I meant. Then, when they had come fully at it, the one who had proposed that they should make spears of their knives, cried out to know why a kite would not do, and at that I was confounded, in that so simple an expedient had not occurred to any before; for, surely, it would be but a little matter to float a line to them by means of a kite, and, further, such a thing would take no great making.

And so, after a space of talk, it was decided that upon the morrow we should build some sort of kite, and with it fly a line over the hulk, the which should be a task of no great difficulty with so good a breeze as we had continually with us.

And, presently, having made our supper off a very fine fish, which the two fishermen had caught whilst we talked, the bo'sun set the watches, and the rest turned-in.

XIII: The Weed Men

Now, on that night, when I came to my watch, I discovered that there was no moon, and, save for such light as the fire threw, the hill-top was in darkness; yet this was no great matter to trouble me; for we had been unmolested since the burning of the fungi in the valley, and thus I had lost much of the haunting fear which had beset me upon the death of Job. Yet, though I was not so much afraid as I had been, I took all precautions that suggested themselves to me, and built up the fire to a goodly height, after which I took my cut-and-thrust, and made the round of the camping place. At the edges of the cliffs which protected us on three sides, I made some pause, staring down into the darkness, and listening; though this latter was of but small use because of the strength of the wind which roared continually in my ears. Yet though I neither saw nor heard anything, I was presently possessed of a strange uneasiness, which made me return twice or thrice to the edge of the cliffs; but always without seeing or hearing anything to justify my superstitions. And so, presently, being determined to give way to no fancifulness, I avoided the boundary of cliffs, and kept more to that part which commanded the slope, up and down which we made our journeys to and from the island below.

Then, it would be near half way through my time of watching, there came to me out of the immensity of weed that lay to leeward, a far distant sound that grew upon my ear, rising and rising into a fearsome scream-ing and shrieking, and then dying away into the distance in queer sobs, and so at last to a note below that of the wind's. At this, as might be supposed, I was somewhat shaken in myself to hear so dread a noise coming out of all that desolation, and then, suddenly, the thought came to me that the screaming was from the ship to leeward of us, and I ran immediately to the edge of the cliff overlooking the weed, and stared into the darkness; but now I perceived, by a light which burned in the hulk, that the screaming had come from some place a great distance to the right of her, and more, as my sense assured me, it could by no means have been pos-sible for those in her to have sent their voices to me against such a breeze as blew at that time.

And so, for a space, I stood nervously pondering, and peering away into the blackness of the night; thus, in a little, I perceived a dull glow upon the horizon, and, presently, there rose into view the upper edge of the moon, and a very welcome sight it was to me; for I had been upon the point of calling the bo'sun to inform him regarding the sound which I had heard; but I had hesitated, being afraid to seem foolish if nothing should befall. Then, even as I stood watching the moon rise into view, there came again to me the beginning of that screaming, somewhat like to the sound of a woman sobbing with a giant's voice, and it grew and strengthened until it pierced through the roar of the wind with an amazing clearness, and then slowly, and seeming to echo and echo, it sank away into the dis-tance, and there was again in my ears no sound beyond that of the wind.

At this, having looked fixedly in the direction from which the sound had proceeded, I ran straightway to the tent and roused the bo'sun; for I had no knowledge of what the noise might portend, and this second cry had shaken from me all my bashfulness. Now the bo'-sun was upon his feet almost before I had made an end of shaking him, and catching up his great cutlass which he kept always by his side, he followed me swiftly out on to the hill-top. Here, I explained to him that I had heard a very fearsome sound which had appeared to proceed out of the vastness of the weed-continent, and that, upon a repetition of the noise, I had decided to call him; for I knew not but that it might signal to us of some coming danger. At that, the bo'sun commended me; though chiding me in that I had hesitated to call him at the first occurrence of the crying, and then, following me to the edge of the leeward cliff, he stood there with me, waiting and listening, perchance there might come again a recurrence of the noise.

For perhaps something over an hour we stood there very silent and listening; but there came to us no sound beyond the continuous noise of the wind, and so, by that time, having grown somewhat impatient of waiting, and the moon being well risen, the bo'sun beckoned to me to make the round of the camp with him. Now, just as I turned away, chancing to look downward at the clear water directly below, I was amazed to see that an innumerable multitude of great fish, like unto those which I had seen on the previous night, were swimming from the weed-continent towards the island. At that, I stepped nearer the edge; for they came so directly towards the island that I expected to see them close in-shore; yet I could not perceive one; for they seemed all of them to vanish at a point some thirty yards distant from the beach, and at that, being amazed both by the numbers of the fish and their strangeness, and the way in which they came on continually, yet never reached the shore, I called to the bo'sun to come and see; for he had gone on a few paces. Upon hearing my call, he came running back; whereat I pointed into the sea below. At that, he stooped forward and peered very intently, and I with him; yet neither one of us could discover the meaning of so curious an exhibition, and so for a while we watched, the bo'sun being quite so much interested as I.

Presently, however, he turned away, saying that we did foolishly to stand here peering at every curious sight, when we should be looking to the welfare of the camp, and so we began to go the round of the hill-top. Now, whilst we had been watching and listening, we had suffered the fire to die down to a most unwise lowness, and consequently, though the moon was rising, there was by no means the same brightness that should have made the camp light. On perceiving this, I went forward to throw some fuel on to the fire, and then, even as I moved, it seemed to me that I saw something stir in the shadow of the tent. And at that, I ran towards the place, uttering a shout, and waving my cut-and-thrust; yet I found nothing, and so, feeling somewhat foolish, I turned to make up the fire, as had been my intention, and whilst I was thus busied, the bo'sun came running over to me to know what I had seen, and in the same instant there ran three of the men out of the tent, all of them waked by my sudden cry. But I had naught to tell them, save that my fancy had played me a trick, and had shown me something where my eyes could find nothing, and at that, two of the men went back to resume their sleep; but the third, the big fellow to whom the bo'sun had given the other cutlass, came with us, bringing his weapon; and, though he kept silent, it seemed to me that he had gathered something of our uneasiness; and for my part I was not sorry to have his company.

Presently, we came to that portion of the hill which

overhung the valley, and I went to the edge of the cliff, intending to peer over; for the valley had a very unholy fascination for me. Yet, no sooner had I glanced down than I started, and ran back to the bo'sun and plucked him by the sleeve, and at that, perceiving my agitation, he came with me in silence to see what matter had caused me so much quiet excitement. Now, when he looked over, he also was astounded, and drew back instantly; then, using great caution, he bent forward once more, and stared down, and, at that, the big sea-man came up behind, walking upon his toes, and stooped to see what manner of thing we had discovered. Thus we each of us stared down upon a most unearthly sight; for the valley all beneath us was a-swarm with moving creatures, white and unwholesome in the moon-light, and their movements were somewhat like the movements of monstrous slugs; though the things them-selves had no resemblance to such in their contours; but minded me of naked humans, very fleshy and crawling upon their stomachs; yet their movements lacked not a surprising rapidity. And now, looking a little over the bo'sun's shoulder, I discovered that these hideous things were coming up out from the pit-like pool in the bottom of the valley, and, suddenly, I was minded of the multitudes of strange fish which we had seen swim-ming towards the island; but which had all disappeared before reaching the shore, and I had no doubt but that they entered the pit through some natural passage known to them beneath the water. And now I was made to understand my thought of the previous night, that I had seen the flicker of tentacles; for these things below us had each two short and stumpy arms; but the ends appeared divided into hateful and wriggling masses of small tentacles, which slid hither and thither as the creatures moved about the bottom of the valley, and at their hinder ends, where they should have grown feet, there seemed other flickering bunches; but it must not be supposed that we saw these things clearly.

Now it is scarcely possible to convey the extraordinary disgust which the sight of these human slugs bred
in me; nor, could I, do I think I would; for were I
successful, then would others be like to retch even as I
did, the spasm coming on without premonition, and
born of very horror. And then, suddenly, even as I
stared, sick with loathing and apprehension, there came
into view, not a fathom below my feet, a face like to the
face which had peered up into my own on that night,
as we drifted beside the weed-continent. At that, I could
have screamed, had I been in less terror; for the great
eyes, so big as crown pieces, the bill like to an inverted
parrot's, and the slug-like undulating of its white and
slimy body, bred in me the dumbness of one mortally
stricken. And, even as I stayed there, my helpless body
bent and rigid, the bo'sun spat a mighty curse into my
ear, and, leaning forward, smote at the thing with his
cutlass; for in the instant that I had seen it, it had ad-
vanced upward by so much as a yard. Now, at this action of the bo'sun's, I came suddenly into possession of
myself, and thrust downward with so much vigour that
I was like to have followed the brute's carcass; for I
overbalanced, and danced giddily for a moment upon
the edge of eternity; and then the bo'sun had me by the
waistband, and I was back in safety; but in that instant
through which I had struggled for my balance, I had
discovered that the face of the cliff was near hid with
the number of the things which were making up to us,
and I turned to the bo'sun, crying out to him that there
were thousands of them swarming up to us. Yet, he
was gone already from me, running towards the fire,
and shouting to the men in the tent to haste to our help
for their very lives, and then he came racing back with
a great armful of the weed, and after him came the
big seaman, carrying a burning tuft from the camp
fire, and so in a few moments we had a blaze, and the
men were bringing more weed; for we had a very good

stock upon the hill-top; for which the Almighty be thanked.

Now, scarce had we lit one fire, when the bo'sun cried out to the big seaman to make another, further along the edge of the cliff, and, in the same instant, I shouted, and ran over to that part of the hill which lay towards the open sea; for I had seen a number of moving things about the edge of the seaward cliff. Now here there was a deal of shadow; for there were scattered certain large masses of rock about this part of the hill, and these held off both the light of the moon, and that from the fires. Here, I came abruptly upon three great shapes moving with stealthiness towards the camp, and, behind these, I saw dimly that there were others. Then, with a loud cry for help, I made at the three, and, as I charged, they rose up on end at me, and I found that they overtopped me, and their vile tentacles were reached out at me. Then I was smiting, and gasping, sick with a sudden stench, the stench of the creatures which I had come already to know. And then something clutched at me, something slimy and vile, and great mandibles champed in my face; but I stabbed upward, and the thing fell from me, leaving me dazed and sick, and smiting weakly. Then there came a rush of feet behind, and a sudden blaze, and the bo'sun crying out encouragement, and, directly, he and the big seaman thrust themselves in front of me, hurling from them great masses of burning weed, which they had borne, each of them, up a long reed. And immediately the things were gone, slithering hastily down over the cliff edge.

And so, presently, I was more my own man, and made to wipe from my throat the slime left by the clutch of the monster: and afterwards I ran from fire to fire with weed, feeding them, and so a space passed, during which we had safety; for by that time we had fires all about the top of the hill, and the monsters were in mortal dread of fire, else had we been dead, all of us, that night.

Now, a while before the dawn, we discovered, for the second time since we had been upon the island, that our fuel could not last us the night at the rate at which we were compelled to burn it, and so the bo'sun told the men to let out every second fire, and thus we staved off for a while the time when we should have to face a spell of darkness, and the things which, at present, the fires held off from us. And so at last, we came to the end of the weed and the reeds, and the bo'sun called out to us to watch the cliff edges very carefully, and smite on the instant that any thing showed; but that, should he call, all were to gather by the central fire for a last stand. And, after that, he blasted the moon which had passed behind a great bank of cloud. And thus matters were, and the gloom deepened as the fires sank lower and lower. Then I heard a man curse, on that part of the hill which lay towards the weed-continent, his cry coming up to me against the wind, and the bo'sun shouted to us to all have a care, and directly afterwards I smote at something that rose silently above the edge of the cliff opposite to where I watched.

Perhaps a minute passed, and then there came shouts from all parts of the hill-top, and I knew that the weed men were upon us, and in the same instant there came two above the edge near me, rising with a ghostly quietness, yet moving lithely. Now the first, I pierced somewhere in the throat, and it fell backward; but the second, though I thrust it through, caught my blade with a bunch of its tentacles, and was like to have snatched it from me; but that I kicked it in the face, and at that, being, I believe, more astonished than hurt, it loosed my sword, and immediately fell away out of sight. Now this had taken, in all, no more than some ten seconds; yet already I perceived so many as four others coming into view a little to my right, and at that it seemed to me that our deaths must be very near, for I knew not how we were to cope with the creatures, coming as they were so boldly and with such rapidity. Yet, I hesitated not, but ran at them, and now I thrust not; but cut at their faces, and found this to be very effectual; for in this wise disposed I of three in as many strokes; but the fourth had come right over the cliff edge, and rose up at me upon its hinder parts, as had done those others when the bo'sun had succoured me. At that, I gave way, having a very lively dread; but, hearing all about me the cries of conflict, and knowing that I could expect no help, I made at the brute: then as it stooped and reached out one of its bunches of tentacles, I sprang back, and slashed at them, and immediately I followed this up by a thrust in the stomach, and at that it collapsed into a writhing white ball, that rolled this way and that, and so, in its agony, coming to the edge of the cliff, it fell over, and I was left, sick and near helpless with the hateful stench of the brutes.

Now by this time all the fires about the edges of the hill were sunken into dull glowing mounds of embers; though that which burnt near to the entrance of the tent was still of a good brightness; yet this helped us but little, for we fought too far beyond the immediate circle of its beams to have benefit of it. And still the moon, at which now I threw a despairing glance, was no more than a ghostly shape behind the great bank of cloud which was passing over it. Then, even as I looked upward, glancing as it might be over my left shoulder, I saw, with a sudden horror, that something had come anigh me, and upon the instant, I caught the reek of the thing, and leapt fearfully to one side, turning as I sprang. Thus was I saved in the very moment of my destruction; for the creature's tentacles smeared the back of my neck as I leapt, and then I had smitten, once and again, and conquered.

Immediately after this, I discovered something to be

crossing the dark space that lay between the dull mound of the nearest fire, and that which lay further along the hill-top, and so, wasting no moment of time, I ran towards the thing, and cut it twice across the head before ever it could get upon its hind parts, in which position I had learned greatly to dread them. Yet, no sooner had I slain this one, than there came a rush of maybe a dozen upon me; these having climbed silently over the cliff edge in the meanwhile. At this, I dodged, and ran madly towards the glowing mound of the nearest fire, the brutes following me almost so quick as I could run; but I came to the fire the first, and then, a sudden thought coming to me, I thrust the point of my cut-and-thrust among the embers and switched a great shower of them at the creatures, and at that I had a momentary clear vision of many white, hideous faces stretched out towards me, and brown, champing mandibles which had the upper beak shutting into the lower; and the clumped, wriggling tentacles were all a-flutter. Then the gloom came again; but immediately, I switched another and yet another shower of the burning embers towards them, and so, directly, I saw them give back, and then they were gone. At this, all about the edges of the hill-top, I saw the fires being scattered in like manner; for others had adopted this device to help them in their sore straits.

For a little after this, I had a short breathing space, the brutes seeming to have taken fright; yet I was full of trembling, and I glanced hither and thither, not knowing when some one or more of them would come upon me. And ever I glanced towards the moon, and prayed the Almighty that the clouds would pass quickly, else should we be all dead men; and then, as I prayed, there rose a sudden very terrible scream from one of the men, and in the same moment there came something over the edge of the cliff fronting me; but I cleft it or ever it could rise higher, and in my ears there echoed still the sudden scream which had come from that part of the hill which lay to the left of me: yet I dared not to leave my station; for to have done so would have been to have risked all, and so I stayed, tortured by the strain of ignorance, and my own terror.

Again, I had a little spell in which I was free from molestation; nothing coming into sight so far as I could see to right or left of me; though others were less fortunate, as the curses and sounds of blows told to me, and then, abruptly, there came another cry of pain, and I looked up again to the moon, and prayed aloud that it might come out to show some light before we were all destroyed; but it remained hid. Then a sudden thought came into my brain, and I shouted at the top of my voice to the bo'sun to set the great cross-bow upon the central fire; for thus we should have a big blaze—the wood being very nice and dry. Twice I shouted to him, saying:—"Burn the bow! Burn the bow!" And immediately he replied, shouting to all the men to run to him and carry it to the fire; and this we did, and bore it to the centre fire, and then ran back with all speed to our places. Thus in a minute we had some light, and the light grew as the fire took hold of the great log, the wind fanning it to a blaze. And so I faced outwards, looking to see if any vile face showed above the edge before me, or to my right or left. Yet, I saw nothing, save, as it seemed to me, once a fluttering tentacle came up, a little to my right; but nothing else for a space.

Perhaps it was near five minutes later, that there came another attack, and, in this, I came near to losing my life, through my folly in venturing too near to the edge of the cliff; for, suddenly, there shot up out from the darkness below, a clump of tentacles, and caught me about the left ankle, and immediately I was pulled to a sitting posture, so that both my feet were over the edge of the precipice, and it was only by the mercy of God that I had not plunged head foremost into the valley. Yet, as it was, I suffered a mighty peril; for the brute that had my foot, put a vast strain upon it, trying to pull me down; but I resisted, using my hands and seat to sustain me, and so, discovering that it could not compass my end in this wise, it slacked somewhat of the stress, and bit at my boot, shearing through the hard leather, and nigh destroying my small toe; but now, being no longer compelled to use both hands to retain my position, I slashed down with great fury, being maddened by the pain and the mortal fear which the creature had put upon me; yet I was not immediately free of the brute; for it caught my sword blade; but I snatched it away before it could take a proper hold, mayhaps cutting its feelers somewhat thereby; though of this I cannot be sure, for they seemed not to grip around a thing, but to *suck* to it; then, in a moment, by a lucky blow, I maimed it, so that it loosed me, and I was able to get back into some condition of security.

And from this onwards, we were free from molestation; though we had no knowledge but that the quietness of the weed men did but portend a fresh attack, and so, at last, it came to the dawn; and in all this time the moon came not to our help, being quite hid by the clouds which now covered the whole arc of the sky, making the dawn of a very desolate aspect.

And so soon as there was a sufficiency of light, we examined the valley; but there were nowhere any of the weed men, no! nor even any of their dead for it seemed that they had carried off all such and their wounded, and so we had no opportunity to make an examination of the monsters by daylight. Yet, though we could not come upon their dead, all about the edges of the cliffs was blood and slime, and from the latter there came ever the hideous stench which marked the brutes; but from this we suffered little, the wind carrying it far away to leeward, and filling our lungs with sweet and wholesome air.

Presently, seeing that the danger was past, the bo'sun

called us to the centre fire, on which burnt still the remnants of the great bow, and here we discovered for the first time that one of the men was gone from us. At that, we made search about the hill-top, and afterwards in the valley and about the island; but found him not.

XIV: In Communication

NOW OF THE SEARCH WHICH WE MADE THROUGH
the valley for the body of Tompkins, that being the
name of the lost man, I have some doleful memories.
But first, before we left the camp, the bo'sun gave us
all a very sound tot of the rum, and also a biscuit
apiece, and thereafter we hasted down, each man holding his weapon readily. Presently, when we were come
to the beach which ended the valley upon the seaward
side, the bo'sun led us along to the bottom of the hill,
where the precipices came down into the softer stuff
which covered the valley, and here we made a careful
search, perchance he had fallen over, and lay dead or
wounded near to our hands. But it was not so, and
after that, we went down to the mouth of the great
pit, and here we discovered the mud all about it to be
covered with multitudes of tracks, and in addition to
these and the slime, we found many traces of blood;
but nowhere any signs of Tompkins. And so, having
searched all the valley, we came out upon the weed
which strewed the shore nearer to the great weed-
continent; but discovered nothing until we had made
up towards the foot of the hill, where it came down
sheer into the sea. Here, I climbed on to a ledge—
the same from which the men had caught their fish—,

thinking that, if Tompkins had fallen from above, he might lie in the water at the foot of the cliff, which was here, maybe, some ten to twenty feet deep; but, for a little space, I saw nothing. Then, suddenly, I discovered that there was something white, down in the sea away to my left, and, at that, I climbed farther out along the ledge.

In this wise I perceived that the thing which had attracted my notice was the dead body of one of the weed men. I could see it but dimly, catching odd glimpses of it as the surface of the water smoothed at whiles. It appeared to me to be lying curled up, and somewhat upon its right side, and in proof that it was dead, I saw a mighty wound that had come near to shearing away the head; and so, after a further glance, I came in, and told what I had seen. At that, being convinced by this time that Tompkins was indeed done to death, we ceased our search; but first, before we left the spot, the bo'sun climbed out to get a sight of the dead weed man and after him the rest of the men for they were greatly curious to see clearly what manner of creature it was that had attacked us in the night. Presently, having seen so much of the brute as the water would allow, they came in again to the beach, and afterwards were returned to the opposite side of the island, and so, being there, we crossed over to the boat, to see whether it had been harmed; but found it to be untouched. Yet, that the creatures had been all about it, we could perceive by the marks of slime upon the sand, and also by the strange trail which they had left in the soft surface. Then one of the men called out that there had been something at Job's grave, which, as will be remembered, had been made in the sand some little distance from the place of our first camp. At that, we looked all of us, and it was easy to see that it had been disturbed, and so we ran hastily to it, knowing not what to fear; thus we found it to be empty; for the monsters had digged down to the poor lad's body, and of it we could discover no sign. Upon this, we came to a greater horror of the weed men than ever; for we knew them now to be foul ghouls who could not let even the dead body rest in the grave.

Now after this, the bo'sun led us all back to the hill-top, and there he looked to our hurts; for one man had lost two fingers in the night's fray; another had been bitten savagely in the left arm; whilst a third had all the skin of his face raised in wheals where one of the brutes had fixed its tentacles. And all of these had received but scant attention, because of the stress of the fight, and, after that, through the discovery that Tompkins was missing. Now, however, the bo'sun set-to upon them, washing and binding them up, and for dressings he made use of some of the oakum which we had with us, binding this on with strips torn from the roll of spare duck, which had been in the locker of the boat.

For my part, seizing this chance to make some examination of my wounded toe, the which, indeed, was causing me to limp, I found that I had endured less harm than seemed to me; for the bone of the toe was untouched, though showing bare; yet when it was cleansed, I had not overmuch pain with it; though I could not suffer to have the boot on, and so bound some canvas about my foot, until such time as it should be healed.

Presently, when our wounds were all attended to, the which had taken time, for there was none of us altogether untouched, the bo'sun bade the man whose fingers were damaged, to lie down in the tent, and the same order he gave also to him that was bitten in the arm. Then, the rest of us he directed to go down with him and carry up fuel; for that the night had shown him how our very lives depended upon a sufficiency of this; and so all that morning we brought fuel to the hill-top, both weed and reeds, resting not until midday, when he gave us a further tot of the rum, and after that set one

of the men upon the dinner. Then he bade the man,
Jessop by name, who had proposed to fly a kite over the
vessel in the weed, to say whether he had any craft in
the making of such a matter. At that, the fellow laughed,
and told the bo'sun that he would make him a kite that
would fly very steadily and strongly, and this without
the aid of a tail. And so the bo'sun bade him set-to
without delay; for that we should do well to deliver the
people in the hulk, and afterwards make all haste from
the island, which was no better than a nesting place of
ghouls.

Now, hearing the man say that his kite would fly
without a tail, I was mightily curious to see what manner of thing he would make; for I had never seen the
like, nor heard that such was possible. Yet he spoke of
no more than he could accomplish; for he took two of
the reeds and cut them to a length of about six feet;
then he bound them together in the middle so that they
formed a Saint Andrew's cross, and after that he made
two more such crosses, and when these were completed,
he took four reeds maybe a dozen feet long, and bade
us stand them upright in the shape of a square, so that
they formed the four corners, and after that he took
one of the crosses, and laid it in the square so that its
four ends touched the four uprights, and in this position he lashed it. Then he took the second cross and
lashed it midway between the top and bottom of the
uprights, and after that he lashed the third at the top, so
that the three of them acted as spreaders to keep the
four longer reeds in their places as though they were for
the uprights of a little square tower. Now, when he had
gotten so far as that, the bo'sun called out to us to make
our dinners, and this we did, and afterwards had a short
time in which to smoke, and whilst we were thus at our
ease the sun came out, the which it had not done all
the day, and at that we felt vastly brighter; for the day
had been very gloomy with clouds until that time, and
what with the loss of Tompkins, and our own fears and

hurts, we had been exceeding doleful; but now, as I have said, we became more cheerful, and went very alertly to the finishing of the kite.

At this point it came suddenly to the bo'sun that we had made no provision of cord for the flying of the kite, and he called out to the man to know what strength the kite would require, at which Jessop answered him that maybe ten-yarn sennit would do, and this being so, the bo'sun led three of us down to the wrecked mast upon the further beach, and from this we stripped all that was left of the shrouds, and carried them to the top of the hill, and so, presently, having unlaid them, we set-to upon the sennit, using ten yarns; but plaiting two as one, by which means we progressed with more speed than if we had taken them singly.

Now, as we worked, I glanced occasionally towards Jessop, and saw that he stitched a band of the light duck around each end of the framework which he had made, and these bands I judged to be about four feet wide, in this wise leaving an open space between the two, so that now the thing looked something like to a Punchinello show, only that the opening was in the wrong place, and there was too much of it. After that he bent on a bridle to two of the uprights, making this of a piece of good hemp rope which he found in the tent, and then he called out to the bo'sun that the kite was finished. At that, the bo'sun went over to examine it, the which did all of us; for none of us had seen the like of such a thing, and, if I misdoubt not, few of us had much faith that it would fly; for it seemed so big and unwieldy. Now, I think that Jessop gathered something of our thoughts; for, calling to one of us to hold the kite, lest it should blow away, he went into the tent, and brought out the remainder of the hemp line, the same from which he had cut the bridle. This, he bent on to it, and, giving the end into our hands, bade us go back with it until all the slack was taken up, he, in the meanwhile, steadying the kite. Then, when we had gone back to the extent of the line, he shouted to us to take a very particular hold upon it, and then, stooping, caught the kite by the bottom, and threw it into the air, whereupon, to our amazement, having swooped somewhat to one side, it steadied and mounted upwards into the sky like a very bird.

Now at this, as I have made mention, we were astonished; for it appeared like a miracle to us to see so cumbrous a thing fly with so much grace and persistence, and further, we were mightily surprised at the manner in which it pulled upon the rope, tugging with such heartiness that we were like to have loosed it in our first astonishment, had it not been for the warning which Jessop called to us.

And now, being well assured of the properness of the kite, the bo'sun bade us to draw it in, the which we did only with difficulty, because of its bigness and the strength of the breeze. And when we had it back again upon the hilltop, Jessop moored it very securely to a great piece of rock, and, after that, having received our approbation, he turned-to with us upon the making of the sennit.

Presently, the evening drawing near, the bo'sun set us to the building of fires about the hill-top, and after that, having waved our goodnights to the people in the hulk, we made our suppers, and lay down to smoke, after which, we turned-to again at our plaiting of the sennit, the which we were in very great haste to have done. And so, later, the dark having come down upon the island, the bo'sun bade us take burning weed from the centre fire, and set light to the heaps of weed that we had stacked round the edges of the hill for that purpose, and so in a few minutes the whole of the hill-top was very light and cheerful, and afterwards, having put two of the men to keep watch and attend to the fires, he sent the rest of us back to our sennit making, keeping us at it until maybe about ten of the clock, after which he arranged that two men at a time should be on watch throughout the night, and then he bade the rest of us turn-in, so soon as he had looked to our various hurts.

Now, when it came to my turn to watch, I discovered that I had been chosen to company the big seaman, at which I was by no means displeased; for he was a most excellent fellow, and moreover a very lusty man to have near, should anything come upon one unawares. Yet, we were happy in that the night passed off without trouble of any sort, and so at last came the morning.

So soon as we had made our breakfast, the bo'sun took us all down to the carrying of fuel; for he saw very clearly that upon a good supply of this depended our immunity from attack. And so for the half of the morning we worked at the gathering of weed and reeds for our fires. Then, when we had obtained a sufficiency for the coming night, he set us all to work again upon the sennit, and so until dinner, after which we turned-to once more upon our plaiting. Yet it was plain that it would take several days to make a sufficient line for our purpose, and because of this, the bo'sun cast about in his mind for some way in which he could quicken its production. Presently, as a result of some little thought, he brought out from the tent the long piece of hemp rope with which we had moored the boat to the sea anchor, and proceeded to unlay it, until he had all three strands separate. Then he bent the three together, and so had a very rough line of maybe some hundred and eighty fathoms in length; yet, though so rough, he judged it strong enough, and thus we had this much the less sennit to make.

Now, presently, we made our dinner, and after that for the rest of the day we kept very steadily to our plaiting, and so, with the previous day's work, had near two hundred fathoms completed by the time that the bo'sun called us to cease and come to supper. Thus it will be seen that counting all, including the piece of hemp line from which the bridle had been made, we may be said to have had at this time about four hundred fathoms towards the length which we needed for our purpose, this having been reckoned at five hundred fathoms.

After supper, having lit all the fires, we continued to work at the plaiting, and so, until the bo'sun set the watches, after which we settled down for the night, first, however, letting the bo'sun see to our hurts. Now this night, like to the previous, brought us no trouble; and when the day came, we had first our breakfast, and then set-to upon our collecting of fuel, after which we spent the rest of the day at the sennit, having manufactured a sufficiency by the evening, the which the bo'sun celebrated by a very rousing tot of the rum. Then, having made our supper, we lit the fires, and had a very comfortable evening, after which, as on the preceding nights, having let the bo'sun attend our wounds, we settled for the night, and on this occasion the bo'sun let the man who had lost his fingers, and the one who had been bitten so badly in the arm, take their first turn at the watching since the night of the attack.

Now when the morning came we were all of us very eager to come to the flying of the kite; for it seemed possible to us that we might effect the rescue of the people in the hulk before the evening. And, at the thought of this, we experienced a very pleasurable sense of excitement; yet, before the bo'sun would let us touch the kite, he insisted that we should gather our usual supply of fuel, the which order, though full of wisdom, irked us exceedingly, because of our eagerness to set about the rescue. But at last this was accomplished, and we made to get the line ready, testing the knots, and seeing that it was all clear for running. Yet, before setting the kite off, the bo'sun took us down to the further beach to bring up the foot of the royal and t'gallant mast, which remained fast to the topmast, and when we had this upon the hill-top, he set its ends upon two rocks, after which he piled a heap of great pieces around them, leaving the middle part clear. Round this he passed the kite line a couple or three times, and then gave the end to Jessop to bend on to the bridle of the kite, and so he had all ready for paying out to the wreck.

And now, having nothing to do, we gathered round to watch, and, immediately, the bo'sun giving the signal, Jessop cast the kite into the air, and, the wind catching it, lifted it strongly and well, so that the bo'sun could scarce pay out fast enough. Now, before the kite had been let go, Jessop had bent to the forward end of it a great length of the spunyarn, so that those in the wreck could catch it as it trailed over them, and, being eager to witness whether they would secure it without trouble, we ran all of us to the edge of the hill to watch. Thus, within five minutes from the time of the loosing of the kite, we saw the people in the ship wave to us to cease veering, and immediately afterwards the kite came swiftly downwards, by which we knew that they had the tripping-line, and were hauling upon it, and at that we gave out a great cheer, and afterwards we sat about and smoked, waiting until they had read our instructions, which we had written upon the covering of the kite.

Presently, maybe the half of an hour afterwards, they signalled to us to haul upon our line, which we proceeded to do without delay, and so, after a great space, we had hauled in all of our rough line, and come upon the end of theirs, which proved to be a fine piece of three-inch hemp, new and very good; yet we could not conceive that this would stand the stress necessary to lift so great a length clear of the weed, as would be needful, or ever we could hope to bring the people of the ship over it in safety. And so we waited some little while, and, presently, they signalled again to us to haul, which we did, and found that they had bent on a much greater rope to the bight of the three-inch hemp, having merely intended the latter for a hauling-line by which to get the heavier rope across the weed to the island. Thus, after a weariful time of pulling, we got the end of the bigger rope up to the hill-top, and discovered it to be an extraordinarily sound rope of some four inches diameter, and smoothly laid of fine yarns round and very true and well spun, and with this we had every reason to be satisfied.

Now to the end of the big rope they had tied a letter, in a bag of oilskin, and in it they said some very warm and grateful things to us, after which they set out a short code of signals by which we should be able to understand one another on certain general matters, and at the end they asked if they should send us any provision ashore; for, as they explained, it would take some little while to get the rope set taut enough for our purpose, and the carrier fixed and in working order. Now, upon reading this letter, we called out to the bo'sun that he should ask them if they would send us some soft bread; the which he added thereto a request for lint and bandages and ointment for our hurts. And this he bade me write upon one of the great leaves from off the reeds, and at the end he told me to ask if they desired us to send them any fresh water. And all of this, I wrote with a sharpened splinter of reed, cutting the words into the surface of the leaf. Then, when I had made an end of writing, I gave the leaf to the bo'sun, and he enclosed it in the oilskin bag, after which he gave the signal for those in the hulk to haul on the smaller line, and this they did.

Presently, they signed to us to pull in again, the which we did, and so, when we had hauled in a great length of their line, we came to the little, oilskin bag, in which we found lint and bandages and ointment, and a further letter, which set out that they were baking bread, and would send us some so soon as it was out from the oven.

Now, in addition to the matters for the healing of our wounds, and the letter, they had included a bundle of paper in loose sheets, some quills and an inkhorn, and at the end of their epistle, they begged very earnestly of us to send them some news of the outer world; for they had been shut up in that strange continent of weed for something over seven years. They told us then that there were twelve of them in the hulk, three of them being women, one of whom had been the captain's wife; but he had died soon after the vessel became entangled in the weed, and along with him more than half of the ship's company, having been attacked by giant devil-fish, as they were attempting to free the vessel from the weed, and afterwards they who were left had built the superstructure as a protection against the devil-fish, and the *devil-men,* as they termed them; for, until it had been built, there had been no safety about the decks, neither day nor night.

To our question as to whether they were in need of water, the people in the ship replied that they had a sufficiency, and, further, that they were very well supplied with provisions; for the ship had sailed from London with a general cargo, among which there was a vast quantity of food in various shapes and forms. At this news we were greatly pleased, seeing that we need have no more anxiety regarding a lack of victuals, and so in the letter which I went into the tent to write, I put down that we were in no great plentitude of provisions, at which hint I guessed they would add somewhat to the bread when it should be ready. And after that I wrote down such chief events as my memory recalled as having occurred in the course of the past seven years, and then, a short account of our own adventures, up to that time, telling them of the attack which we had suffered from the weed men, and asking such questions as my curiosity and wonder prompted.

Now whilst I had been writing, sitting in the mouth of the tent, I had observed, from time to time, how that the bo'sun was busied with the men in passing the end of the big rope round a mighty boulder, which lay about ten fathoms in from the edge of the cliff which overlooked the hulk. This he did, parcelling the rope where the rock was in any way sharp, so as to protect it from being cut; for which purpose he made use of some of the canvas. And by the time that I had the letter completed, the rope was made very secure to the great piece of rock, and, further, they had put a large piece of chafing gear under that part of the rope where it took the edge of the cliff.

Now having, as I have said, completed the letter, I went out with it to the bo'sun; but, before placing it in the oilskin bag, he bade me add a note at the bottom, to say that the big rope was all fast, and that they could heave on it so soon as it pleased them, and after that we dispatched the letter by means of the small line, the men in the hulk hauling it off to them so soon as they perceived our signals.

By this, it had come well on to the latter part of the afternoon, and the bo'sun called us to make some sort of a meal, leaving one man to watch the hulk, perchance they should signal to us. For we had missed our dinner in the excitement of the day's work, and were come now to feel the lack of it. Then, in the midst of it, the man upon the look-out cried out that they were signalling to us from the ship, and, at that, we ran all of us to see what they desired, and so, by the code which we had arranged between us, we found that they waited for us to haul upon the small line. This did we, and made out presently that we were hauling something across the weed, of a very fair bulk, at which we warmed to our work, guessing that it was the bread which they had promised us, and so it proved, and done up with great neatness in a long roll of tarpaulin, which had been wrapped around both the loaves and the rope, and lashed very securely at the ends, thus producing a taper shape convenient for passing over the weed without catching. Now, when we came to open this parcel, we discovered that my hint had taken very sound effect; for there were in the parcel, besides the loaves, a boiled ham, a Dutch cheese, two bottles of port well padded from breakage, and four pounds of tobacco in plugs. And at this coming of good things, we stood all of us upon the edge of the hill, and waved our thanks to those in the ship, they waving back in all good will, and after that we went back to our meal, at which we sampled the new victuals with very lusty appetites.

There was in the parcel, one other matter, a letter, most neatly indited, as had been the former epistles, in a feminine hand-writing, so that I guessed they had one of the women to be their scribe. This epistle answered some of my queries, and, in particular, I remember that it informed me as to the probable cause of the strange crying which preceded the attack by the weed men, saying that on each occasion when they in the ship had suffered their attacks, there had been always this same crying, being evidently a summoning call or signal to the attack, though how given, the writer had not discovered; for the weed *devils*—this being how they in the ship spoke always of them—made never a sound when attacking, not even when wounded to the death, and, indeed, I may say here, that we never learnt the way in which that lonesome sobbing was produced, nor, indeed, did they, or we, discover more than the merest tithe of the mysteries which that great continent of weed holds in its silence.

Another matter to which I had referred was the consistent blowing of the wind from one quarter, and this the writer told me happened for as much as six months in the year, keeping up a very steady strength. A further thing there was which gave me much interest; it was that the ship had not been always where we had discovered her; for at one time they had been so far within the weed, that they could scarce discern the open sea upon the far horizon; but that at times the weed opened in great gulfs that went yawning through the continent for scores of miles, and in this way the shape and coasts of the weed were being constantly altered; these happenings being for the most part at the change of the wind.

And much more there was that they told us then and afterwards, how that they dried weed for their fuel, and how the rains, which fell with great heaviness at certain periods, supplied them with fresh water; though, at times, running short, they had learnt to distil sufficient for their needs until the next rains.

Now, near to the end of the epistle, there came some news of their present actions, and thus we learnt that they in the ship were busy at staying the stump of the mizzen-mast, this being the one to which they proposed to attach the big rope, taking it through a great iron-bound snatch-block, secured to the head of the stump, and then down to the mizzen-capstan, by which, and a strong tackle, they would be able to heave the line so taut as was needful.

Now, having finished our meal, the bo'sun took out the lint, bandages and ointment, which they had sent us from the hulk, and proceeded to dress our hurts, beginning with him who had lost his fingers, which, happily, were making a very healthy heal. And afterwards we went all of us to the edge of the cliff, and sent back the look-out to fill such crevices in his stomach as remained yet empty; for we had passed him already some sound hunks of the bread and ham and cheese, to eat whilst he kept watch, and so he had suffered no great harm.

It may have been near an hour after this, that the bo'sun pointed out to me that they in the ship had commenced to heave upon the great rope, and so I perceived, and stood watching it; for I knew that the bo'sun had some anxiety as to whether it would take-up sufficiently clear of the weed to allow those in the ship to be hauled along it, free from molestation by the great devil-fish.

Presently, as the evening began to draw on, the

bo'sun bade us go and build our fires about the hill-top, and this we did, after which we returned to learn how the rope was lifting, and now we perceived that it had come clear of the weed, at which we felt mightily rejoiced, and waved encouragement, chance there might be any who watched us from the hulk. Yet, though the rope was up clear of the weed, the bight of it had to rise to a much greater height, or ever it would do for the purpose for which we intended it, and already it suffered a vast strain, as I discovered by placing my hand upon it; for, even to lift the slack of so great a length of line meant the stress of some tons. And later I saw that the bo'sun was growing anxious; for he went over to the rock around which he had made fast the rope, and examined the knots, and those places where he had parcelled it, and after that he walked to the place where it went over the edge of the cliff, and here he made a further scrutiny; but came back presently, seeming not dissatisfied.

Then, in a while, the darkness came down upon us, and we lighted our fires and prepared for the night, having the watches arranged as on the preceding nights.

XV: Aboard the Hulk

NOW WHEN IT CAME TO MY WATCH, THE WHICH I TOOK
in company with the big seaman, the moon had not yet
risen, and all the island was vastly dark, save the hill-
top, from which the fires blazed in a score of places,
and very busy they kept us, supplying them with fuel.
Then, when maybe the half of our watch had passed,
the big seaman, who had been to feed the fires upon the
weed side of the hill-top, came across to me, and bade
me come and put my hand upon the lesser rope; for that
he thought they in the ship were anxious to haul it in so
that they might send some message across to us. At his
words, I asked him very anxiously whether he had perceived them waving a light, the which we had arranged
to be our method of signalling in the night, in the event
of such being needful; but, to this, he said that he had
seen naught; and, by now, having come near the edge
of the cliff, I could see for myself, and so perceived that
there was none signalling to us from the hulk. Yet, to
please the fellow, I put my hand upon the line, which
we had made fast in the evening to a large piece of
rock, and so, immediately, I discovered that something
was pulling upon it, hauling and then slackening, so
that it occurred to me that the people in the vessel might
be indeed wishful to send us some message, and at that,

142

to make sure, I ran to the nearest fire, and, lighting a tuft of weed, waved it thrice; but there came not any answering signal from those in the ship, and at that I went back to feel at the rope, to assure myself that it had not been the pluck of the wind upon it; but I found that it was something very different from the wind, something that plucked with all the sharpness of a hooked fish, only that it had been a mighty great fish to have given such tugs, and so I knew that some vile thing out in the darkness of the weed was fast to the rope, and at this there came the fear that it might break it, and then a second thought that something might be climbing up to us along the rope, and so I bade the big seaman stand ready with his great cutlass, whilst I ran and waked the bo'sun. And this I did, and explained to him how that something meddled with the lesser rope, so that he came immediately to see for himself how this might be, and when he had put his hand upon it, he bade me go and call the rest of the men, and let them stand round by. the fires; for that there was something abroad in the night, and we might be in danger of attack; but he and the big seaman stayed by the end of the rope, watching, so for as the darkness would allow, and ever and anon feeling the tension upon it.

Then, suddenly, it came to the bo'sun to look to the second line, and he ran, cursing himself for his thoughtlessness; but because of its greater weight and tension, he could not discover for certain whether anything meddled with it or not; yet he stayed by it, arguing that if aught touched the smaller rope then might something do likewise with the greater, only that the small line lay along the weed, whilst the greater one had been some feet above it when the darkness had fallen over us, and so might be free from any prowling creatures.

And thus, maybe, an hour passed, and we kept watch and tended the fires, going from one to another, and, presently, coming to that one which was nearest to the bo'sun, I went over to him, intending to pass a few

minutes in talk; but as I drew nigh to him, I chanced to
place my hand upon the big rope, and at that I ex-
claimed in surprise; for it had become much slacker
than when last I had felt it in the evening, and I asked
the bo'sun whether he had noticed it, whereat he felt
the rope, and was almost more amazed than I had been;
for when last he had touched it, it had been taut, and
humming in the wind. Now, upon this discovery, he
was in much fear that something had bitten through it,
and called to the men to come all of them and pull
upon the rope, so that he might discover whether it
was indeed parted; but when they came and hauled
upon it, they were unable to gather in any of it, whereat
we felt all of us mightily relieved in our minds; though
still unable to come at the cause of its sudden slackness.

And so, a while later, there rose the moon, and we
were able to examine the island and the water between
it and the weed-continent, to see whether there was anything stirring; yet neither in the valley, nor on the faces
of the cliffs, nor in the open water could we perceive
aught living, and as for anything among the weed, it was
small use trying to discover it among all that shaggy
blackness. And now, being assured that nothing was
coming at us, and that, so far as our eyes could pierce,
there climbed nothing upon the ropes, the bo'sun bade
us get turned-in, all except those whose time it was to
watch. Yet, before I went into the tent, I made a careful
examination of the big rope, the which did also the
bo'sun, but could perceive no cause for its slackness;
though this was quite apparent in the moonlight, the
rope going down with greater abruptness than it had
done in the evening. And so we could but conceive that
they in the hulk had slacked it for some reason; and
after that we went to the tent and a further spell of
sleep.

In the early morning we were waked by one of the
watchmen, coming into the tent to call the bo'sun; for it
appeared that the hulk had moved in the night, so that

its stern was now pointed somewhat towards the island. At this news, we ran all of us from the tent to the edge of the hill, and found it to be indeed as the man had said, and now I understood the reason of that sudden slackening of the rope; for, after withstanding the stress upon it for some hours, the vessel had at last yielded, and slewed its stern towards us, moving also to some extent bodily in our direction.

And now we discovered that a man in the look-out place in the top of the structure was waving a wel-come to us, at which we waved back, and then the bo'sun bade me haste and write a note to know whether it seemed to them likely that they might be able to heave the ship clear of the weed, and this I did, greatly excited within myself at this new thought, as, indeed, was the bo'sun himself and the rest of the men. For could they do this, then how easily solved were every problem of coming to our own country. But it seemed too good a thing to have come true, and yet I could but hope. And so, when my letter was com-pleted, we put it up in the little oilskin bag, and sig-nalled to those in the ship to haul in upon the line. Yet, when they went to haul, there came a mighty splather amid the weed, and they seemed unable to gather in any of the slack, and then, after a cer-tain pause, I saw the man in the look-out point some-thing, and immediately afterwards there belched out in front of him a little puff of smoke, and, presently, I caught the report of a musket, so that I knew that he was firing at something in the weed. He fired again, and yet once more, and after that they were able to haul in upon the line, and so I perceived that his fire had proved effectual; yet we had no knowledge of the thing at which he had discharged his weapon.

Now, presently, they signalled to us to draw back the line, the which we could do only with great difficulty, and then the man in the top of the super-structure signed to us to vast hauling, which we did, whereupon he began to fire again into the weed; though with what effect we could not perceive. Then, in a while he signalled to us to haul again, and now the rope came more easily; yet still with much labour, and a commotion in the weed over which it lay and, in places, sank. And so, at last, as it cleared the weed because of the lift of the cliff, we saw that a great crab had clutched it, and that we hauled it towards us; for the creature had too much obstinacy to let go.

Perceiving this, and fearing that the great claws of the crab might divide the rope, the bo'sun caught up one of the men's lances, and ran to the cliff edge, calling to us to pull in gently, and put no more strain upon the line than need be. And so, hauling with great steadiness, we brought the monster near to the edge of the hill, and there, at a wave from the bo'sun, stayed our pulling. Then he raised the spear, and smote at the creature's eyes, as he had done on a previous occasion, and immediately it loosed its hold, and fell with a mighty splash into the water at the foot of the cliff. Then the bo'sun bade us haul in the rest of the rope, until we should come to the packet, and, in the meantime, he examined the line to see whether it had suffered harm through the mandibles of the crab; yet, beyond a little chafe, it was quite sound.

And so we came to the letter, which I opened and read, finding it to be written in the same feminine hand which had indited the others. From it we gathered that the ship had burst through a very thick mass of the weed which had compacted itself about her, and that the second mate, who was the only officer remaining to them, thought there might be good chance to heave the vessel out; though it would have to be done with great slowness, so as to allow the weed to part gradually, otherwise the ship would but act as a gigantic rake to gather up weed before it, and so form its own barrier to clear water. And after this there were kind wishes and hopes that we had spent a good night, the which I took to be prompted by the feminine heart of the writer, and after that I fell to wondering whether it was the captain's wife who acted as scribe. Then I was waked from my pondering, by one of the men crying out that they in the ship had commenced to heave again upon the big rope, and, for a time, I stood and watched it rise slowly, as it came to tautness.

I had stood there awhile, watching the rope, when, suddenly, there came a commotion amid the weed, about two-thirds of the way to the ship, and now I saw that the rope had freed itself from the weed, and, clutching it, were, maybe, a score of giant crabs. At this sight, some of the men cried out their astonishment, and then we saw that there had come a number of men into the look-out place in the top of the superstructure, and, immediately, they opened a very brisk fire upon the creatures, and so, by ones and twos they fell back into the weed, and after that, the men in the hulk resumed their heaving, and so, in a while, had the rope some feet clear of the surface.

Now, having tautened the rope so much as they thought proper, they left it to have its due effect upon the ship, and proceeded to attach a great block to it; then they signalled to us to slack away on the little rope until they had the middle part of it, and this they hitched around the neck of the block, and to the eye in the strop of the block they attached a bo'sun's chair, and so they had ready a carrier, and by this means we were able to haul stuff to and from the hulk without having to drag it across the surface of the weed; being, indeed, the fashion in which we had intended to haul ashore the people in the ship. But now we had the bigger project of salving the ship herself, and, further, the big rope, which acted as support for the carrier, was not yet of a sufficient height above the weed-continent for it to be safe to attempt to bring any ashore by such means; and now that we had hopes of saving the ship, we did not intend to risk parting the big rope, by trying to attain such a degree of tautness as would have been necessary at this time to have raised its bight to the desired height.

Now, presently, the bo'sun called out to one of the men to make breakfast, and when it was ready we came to it, leaving the man with the wounded arm to keep watch; then when we had made an end, he sent him, that had lost his fingers, to keep a look-out whilst the other came to the fire and ate his breakfast. And in the meanwhile, the bo'sun took us down to collect weed and reeds for the night, and so we spent the greater part of the morning, and when we had made an end of this, we returned to the top of the hill, to discover how matters were going forward; thus we found, from the one at the look-out, that they, in the hulk, had been obliged to heave twice upon the big rope to keep it off the weed, and by this we knew that the ship was indeed making a slow sternway towards the island—slipping steadily through the weed, and as we looked at her, it seemed almost that we could perceive that she was nearer; but this was no more than imagination; for, at most, she could not have moved more than some odd fathoms. Yet it cheered us greatly, so that we waved our congratulations to the man who stood in the look-out in the superstructure, and he waved back.

Later, we made dinner, and afterwards had a very comfortable smoke, and then the bo'sun attended to our various hurts. And so through the afternoon we sat about upon the crest of the hill overlooking the hulk, and thrice had they in the ship to heave upon the big rope, and by evening they had made near thirty fathoms towards the island, the which they told us in reply to a query which the bo'sun desired me to send them, several messages having passed between us in the course of the afternoon, so that we had the carrier upon our side. Further than this, they explained that they would tend the rope during the night, so that the strain would be kept up, and, more, this would keep the ropes off the weed.

And so, the night coming down upon us, the bo'sun bade us light the fires about the top of the hill, the same having been laid earlier in the day, and thus, our supper having been dispatched, we prepared for the night. And all through it there burned lights aboard the hulk, the which proved very companionable to us in our times of watching; and so, at last came the morning, the darkness having passed without event. And now, to our huge pleasure, we discovered that the ship had made great progress in the night; being now so much nearer that none could suppose it a matter of imagination; for she must have moved nigh sixty fathoms nearer to the island, so that now we seemed able almost to recognize the face of the man in the look-out; and many things about the hulk we saw with greater clearness, so that we scanned her with a fresh interest. Then the man in the look-out waved a morning greeting to us, the which we returned very heartily, and, even as we did so, there came a second figure beside the man, and waved some white matter, perchance a handkerchief, which is like enough, seeing that it was a woman, and at that, we took off our head coverings, all of us, and shook them at her, and after this we went to our breakfast; having finished which, the bo'sun dressed our hurts, and then, setting the man, who had lost his fingers, to watch, he took the rest of us, excepting him that was bitten in the arm, down to collect fuel, and so the time passed until near dinner.

When we returned to the hill-top, the man upon the look-out told us that they in the ship had heaved not less than four separate times upon the big rope, the which, indeed, they were doing at that present minute; and it was very plain to see that the ship had come nearer even during the short space of the morning. Now, when they had made an end of tautening the rope, I perceived that it was, at last, well clear of the weed through all its length, being at its lowest part nigh twenty feet above the surface, and, at that, a sudden thought came to me which sent me hastily to the bo'sun; for it had occurred to me that there existed no reason why we should not pay a visit to those aboard the hulk. But when I put the matter to him, he shook his head, and, for awhile, stood out against my desire; but, presently, having examined the rope, and considering that I was the lightest of any in the island, he consented, and at that I ran to the carrier which had been hauled across to our side, and got me into the chair. Now, the men, so soon as they perceived my intention, applauded me very heartily, desiring to follow; but the bo'sun bade them be silent, and, after that, he lashed me into the chair, with his own hands, and then signalled to those in the ship to haul upon the small rope; he, in the meanwhile, checking my descent towards the weeds, by means of our end of the hauling-line.

And so, presently, I had come to the lowest part, where the bight of the rope dipped downward in a bow towards the weed, and rose again to the mizzen mast of the hulk. Here I looked downward with somewhat fearful eyes; for my weight on the rope made it sag somewhat lower than seemed to me comfortable, and I had a very lively recollection of some of the horrors which that quiet surface hid. Yet I was not long in this place; for they in the ship, perceiving how the rope let me nearer to the weed than was safe, pulled very heartily upon the hauling-line, and so I came quickly to the hulk.

Now, as I drew nigh to the ship, the men crowded upon a little platform which they had built in the superstructure somewhat below the broken head of the mizzen, and here they received me with loud cheers and very open arms, and were so eager to get me out of the bo'sun's chair, that they cut the lashings, being too impatient to cast them loose. Then they led me down to

the deck, and here, before I had knowledge of aught
else, a very buxom woman took me into her arms, kiss-
ing me right heartily, at which I was greatly taken
aback; but the men about me did naught but laugh, and
so, in a minute, she loosed me, and there I stood, not
knowing whether to feel like a fool or a hero; but in-
clining rather to the latter. Then, at this minute, there
came a second woman, who bowed to me in a manner
most formal, so that we might have been met in some
fashionable gathering, rather than in a cast-away hulk
in the lonesomeness and terror of that weed-choked sea;
and at her coming all the mirth of the men died out of
them, and they became very sober, whilst the buxom
woman went backward for a piece, and seemed somewhat abashed. Now, at all this, I was greatly puzzled,
and looked from one to another to learn what it might
mean; but in the same moment the woman bowed
again, and said something in a low voice touching the
weather, and after that she raised her glance to my face,
so that I saw her eyes, and they were so strange and
full of melancholy, that I knew on the instant why she
spoke and acted in so unmeaning a way; for the poor
creature was out of her mind, and when I learnt afterwards that she was the captain's wife, and had seen
him die in the arms of a mighty devil-fish, I grew to
understand how she had come to such a pass.

Now for a minute after I had discovered the woman's
madness, I was so taken aback as to be unable to answer her remark; but for this there appeared no necessity; for she turned away and went aft towards the
saloon stairway, which stood open, and here she was
met by a maid very bonny and fair, who led her tender-
ly down from my sight. Yet, in a minute, this same maid
appeared, and ran along the decks to me, and caught
my two hands, and shook them, and looked up at me
with such roguish, playful eyes, that she warmed my
heart, which had been strangely chilled by the greeting

of the poor mad woman. And she said many hearty things regarding my courage, to which I knew in my heart I had no claim; but I let her run on, and so, presently, coming more to possession of herself, she discovered that she was still holding my hands, the which, indeed, I had been conscious of the while with a very great pleasure; but at her discovery she dropped them with haste, and stood back from me a space, and so there came a little coolness into her talk: yet this lasted not long; for we were both of us young; and, I think, even thus early we attracted one the other; though, apart from this, there was so much that we desired each to learn, that we could not but talk freely, asking question for question, and giving answer for answer. And thus a time passed, in which the men left us alone, and went presently to the capstan, about which they had taken the big rope, and at this they toiled awhile; for already the ship had moved sufficiently to let the line fall slack.

Presently, the maid, whom I had learnt was niece to the captain's wife, and named Mary Madison, proposed to take me the round of the ship, to which proposal I agreed very willingly; but first I stopped to examine the mizzen stump, and the manner in which the people of the ship had stayed it, the which they had done very cunningly, and I noted how that they had removed some of the superstructure from about the head of the mast, so as to allow passage for the rope, without putting a strain upon the superstructure itself. Then when I had made an end upon the poop, she led me down on to the main-deck, and here I was very greatly impressed by the prodigious size of the structure which they had built about the hulk, and the skill with which it had been carried out, the supports crossing from side to side and to the decks in a manner calculated to give great solidity to that which they upheld. Yet, I was very greatly puzzled to know where they had gotten a sufficiency of timber to make so large a matter; but upon this point she satisfied me by explaining that they had taken up the 'tween decks, and used all such bulkheads as they could spare, and, further, that there had been a good deal among the dunnage which had proved usable.

And so we came at last to the galley, and here I discovered the buxom woman to be installed as cook, and there were in with her a couple of fine children, one of whom I guessed to be a boy of maybe some five years, and the second a girl, scarce able to do more than toddle. At this I turned and asked Mistress Madison whether these were her cousins; but in the next moment I remembered that they could not be; for, as I knew, the captain had been dead some seven years; yet it was the woman in the galley who answered my question; for she turned and, with something of a red face, informed me that they were hers, at which I felt some surprise; but supposed that she had taken passage in the ship with her husband; yet in this I was not correct; for she proceeded to explain that, thinking they were cut off from the world for the rest of this life, and falling very fond of the carpenter, they had made it up together to make a sort of marriage, and had gotten the second mate to read the service over them. She told me then, how that she had taken passage with her mistress, the captain's wife, to help her with her niece, who had been but a child when the ship sailed; for she had been very attached to them both, and they to her. And so she came to an end of her story, expressing a hope that she had done no wrong by her marriage, as none had been intended. And to this I made answer, assuring her that no decent-minded man could think the worse of her; but that I, for my part, thought rather the better, seeing that I liked the pluck which she had shown. At that she cast down the soup ladle, which she had in her fist, and came towards me, wiping her hands; but I gave back, for I shamed to be hugged again, and before

Mistress Mary Madison, and at that she came to a stop and laughed very heartily; but, all the same, called down a very warm blessing upon my head; for which I had no cause to feel the worse. And so I passed on with the captain's niece.

Presently, having made the round of the hulk, we came aft again to the poop, and discovered that they were heaving once more upon the big rope, the which was very heartening, proving, as it did, that the ship was still a-move. And so, a little later, the girl left me, having to attend to her aunt. Now whilst she was gone, the men came all about me, desiring news of the world beyond the weed-continent, and so for the next hour I was kept very busy, answering their questions. Then the second mate called out to them to take another heave upon the rope, and at that they turned to the capstan, and I with them, and so we hove it taut again, after which they got about me once more, questioning; for so much seemed to have happened in the seven years in which they had been imprisoned. And then, after a while, I turned-to and questioned them on such points as I had neglected to ask Mistress Madison, and they discovered to me their terror and sickness of the weed-continent, its desolation and horror, and the dread which had beset them at the thought that they should all of them come to their ends wihout sight of their homes and countrymen.

Now, about this time, I became conscious that I had grown very empty; for I had come off to the hulk before we had made our dinner, and had been in such interest since, that the thought of food had escaped me; for I had seen none eating in the hulk, they, without doubt, having dined earlier than my coming. But now, being made aware of my state by the grumbling of my stomach, I inquired whether there was any food to be had at such a time, and, at that, one of the men ran to tell the woman in the galley that I had missed my dinner, at which she made much ado, and set-to and prepared me a very good meal, which she carried aft and set out for me in the saloon, and after that she sent me down to it.

Presently, when I had come near to being comfortable, there chanced a lightsome step upon the floor behind me, and, turning, I discovered that Mistress Madison was surveying me with a roguish and somewhat amused air. At that, I got hastily to my feet; but she bade me sit down, and therewith she took a seat opposite, and so bantered me with a gentle playfulness that was not displeasing to me, and at which I played so good a second as I had ability. Later, I fell to questioning her, and, among other matters, discovered that it was she who acted as scribe for the people in the hulk, at which I told her that I had done likewise for those on the island. After that, our talk became somewhat personal, and I learnt that she was near on to nineteen years of age, whereat I told her that I had passed my twenty-third. And so we chatted on, until, presently, it occurred to me that I had better be preparing to return to the island, and I rose to my feet with this intention; yet feeling that I had been very much happier to have stayed, the which I thought, for a moment, had not been displeasing to her, and this I imagined, noting somewhat in her eyes when I made mention that I must be gone. Yet it may be that I flattered myself.

Now when I came out on deck, they were busied again in heaving taut the rope, and, until they had made an end, Mistress Madison and I filled the time with such chatter as is wholesome between a man and maid who have not long met, yet find one another pleasing company. Then, when at last the rope was taut, I went up to the mizzen staging, and climbed into the chair, after which some of the men lashed me in very securely. Yet when they gave the signal to haul me to the island, there came for awhile no response, and then signs that we could not understand; but no movement to haul me across the weed. At that, they unlashed me from the chair, bidding me get out, whilst they sent a message to discover what might be wrong. And this they did, and, presently, there came back word that the big rope had stranded upon the edge of the cliff, and that they must slacken it somewhat at once, the which they did, with many expressions of dismay. And so, maybe an hour passed, during which we watched the men working at the rope, just where it came down over the edge of the hill, and Mistress Madison stood with us and watched; for it was very terrible, this sudden thought of failure (though it were but temporary) when they were so near to success. Yet, at last there came a signal from the island for us to loose the hauling-line, the which we did, allowing them to haul across the carrier, and so, in a little while, they signalled back to us to pull in, which, having done, we found a letter in the bag lashed to the carrier, in which the bo'sun made it plain that he had strengthened the rope, and placed fresh chafing gear about it, so that he thought it would be so safe as ever to heave upon; but to put it to a less strain. Yet he refused to allow me to venture across upon it, saying that I must stay in the ship until we were clear of the weed; for if the rope had stranded in one place, then had it been so cruelly tested that there might be some other points at which it was ready to give. And this final note of the bo'sun's made us all very serious; for, indeed, it seemed possible that it was as he suggested; yet they reassured themselves by pointing out that, like enough, it had been the chafe upon the cliff edge which had frayed the strand, so that it had been weakened before it parted; but I, remembering the chafing gear which the bo'sun had put about it in the first instance, felt not so sure; yet I would not add to their anxieties.

And so it came about that I was compelled to spend the night in the hulk; but, as I followed Mistress Madison into the big saloon, I felt no regret, and had near forgotten already my anxiety regarding the rope.

And out on deck there sounded most cheerily the clack of the capstan.

XVI: Freed

Now, when Mistress Madison had seated herself, she invited me to do likewise, after which we fell into talk, first touching upon the matter of the stranding of the rope, about which I hastened to assure her, and later to other things, and so, as is natural enough with a man and maid, to ourselves, and here we were very content to let it remain.

Presently, the second mate came in with a note from the bo'sun, which he laid upon the table for the girl to read, the which she beckoned me to do also, and so I discovered that it was a suggestion, written very rudely and ill-spelt, that they should send us a quantity of reeds from the island, with which we might be able to ease the weed somewhat from around the stern of the hulk, thus aiding her progress. And to this the second mate desired the girl to write a reply, saying that we should be very happy for the reeds, and would endeavour to act upon his hint, and this Mistress Madison did, after which she passed the letter to me, perchance I desired to send any message. Yet I had naught that I wished to say, and so handed it back, with a word of thanks, and, at once, she gave it to the second mate, who went, forthwith, and dispatched it.

Later, the stout woman from the galley came aft to

set out the table, which occupied the centre of the
saloon, and whilst she was at this, she asked for information on many things, being very free and unaffected
in her speech, and seeming with less of deference to my
companion, than a certain motherliness; for it was very
plain that she loved Mistress Madison, and in this my
heart did not blame her. Further, it was plain to me
that the girl had a very warm affection for her old
nurse, which was but natural, seeing that the old woman had cared for her through all the past years, besides being companion to her, and a good and cheerful
one, as I could guess.

Now awhile I passed in answering the buxom woman's questions, and odd times such occasional ones as
were slipt in by Mistress Madison; and then, suddenly
there came the clatter of men's feet overhead, and, later,
the thud of something being cast down upon the deck,
and so we knew that the reeds had come. At that, Mistress Madison cried out that we should go and watch
the men try them upon the weed; for that if they proved
of use in easing that which lay in our path, then
should we come the more speedily to the clear water,
and this without the need of putting so great a strain
upon the hawser, as had been the case hitherto.

When we came to the poop, we found the men re-
moving a portion of the superstructure over the stern,
and after that they took some of the stronger reeds,
and proceeded to work at the weed that stretched away
in a line with our taffrail. Yet that they anticipated danger, I perceived; for there stood by them two of the men
and the second mate, all armed with muskets, and these
three kept a very strict watch upon the weed, knowing,
through much experience of its terrors, how that there
might be a need for their weapons at any moment. And
so a while passed, and it was plain that the men's work
upon the weed was having effect; for the rope grew
slack visibly, and those at the capstan had all that they
could do, taking fleet and fleet with the tackle, to

keep it anywhere near to tautness, and so, perceiving that they were kept so hard at it, I ran to give a hand, the which did Mistress Madison, pushing upon the capstan-bars right merrily and with heartiness. And thus a while passed, and the evening began to come down upon the lonesomeness of the weed-continent. Then there appeared the buxom woman, and bade us come to our suppers, and her manner of addressing the two of us was the manner of one who might have mothered us; but Mistress Madison cried out to her to wait, that we had found work to do, and at that the big woman laughed, and came towards us threateningly, as though intending to remove us hence by force.

And now, at this moment, there came a sudden interruption which checked our merriment; for, abruptly, there sounded the report of a musket in the stern, and then came shouts, and the noise of the two other weapons, seeming like thunder, being pent by the over-arching superstructure. And, directly, the men about the taffrail gave back, running here and there, and so I saw that great arms had come all about the opening which they had made in the superstructure, and two of these flickered in-board, searching hither and thither; but the stout woman took a man near to her, and thrust him out of danger, and after that, she caught Mistress Madison up in her big arms, and ran down on to the main-deck with her, and all this before I had come to a full knowledge of our danger. But now I perceived that I should do well to get further back from the stern, the which I did with haste, and, coming to a safe position, I stood and stared at the huge creature, its great arms, vague in the growing dusk, writhing about in vain search for a victim. Then returned the second mate, having been for more weapons, and now I observed that he armed all the men, and had brought up a spare musket for my use, and so we commenced, all of us, to fire at the monster, whereat it began to lash about most furiously, and so, after some minutes, it slipped away from the opening and slid down into the weed. Upon that several of the men rushed to replace those parts of the superstructure which had been removed, and I with them; yet there were sufficient for the job, so that I had no need to do aught; thus, before they had made up the opening, I had been given chance to look out upon the weed, and so discovered that all the surface which lay between our stern and the island, was moving in vast ripples, as though mighty fish were swimming beneath it, and then, just before the men put back the last of the great panels, I saw the weed all tossed up like to a vast pot a-boil, and then a vague glimpse of thousands of monstrous arms that filled the air, and came towards the ship.

And then the men had the panel back in its place, and were hasting to drive the supporting struts into their positions. And when this was done, we stood awhile and listened; but there came no sound above that of the wail of the wind across the extent of the weed-continent. And at that, I turned to the men, asking how it was that I could hear no sounds of the creatures attacking us, and so they took me up into the look-out place, and from there I stared down at the weed; but it was without movement, save for the stirring of the wind, and there was nowhere any sign of the devil-fish. Then, seeing me amazed, they told me how that anything which moved the weed seemed to draw them from all parts; but that they seldom touched the hulk unless there was something visible to them which had movement. Yet, as they went on to explain, there would be hundreds and hundreds of them lying all about the ship, hiding in the weed; but that, if we took care not to show ourselves within their reach, they would have gone most of them by the morning. And this the men told me in a very matter-of-fact way; for they had become inured to such happenings.

Presently, I heard Mistress Madison calling to me by name, and so descended out of the growing darkness, to the interior of the superstructure, and here they had lit a number of rude slush-lamps, the oil for which, as I learned later, they obtained from a certain fish which haunted the sea, beneath the weed, in very large schools, and took near any sort of bait with great readiness. And so, when I had climbed down into the light, I found the girl waiting for me to come to supper, for which I discovered myself to be in a mightily agreeable humour.

Presently, having made an end of eating, she leaned back in her seat and commenced once more to bait me in her playful manner, the which appeared to afford her much pleasure, and in which I joined with no less, and so we fell presently to more earnest talk, and in this wise we passed a great space of the evening. Then there came to her a sudden idea, and what must she do but propose that we should climb to the look-out, and to this I agreed with a very happy willingness. And to the look-out we went. Now when we had come there, I perceived her reason for this freak; for away in the night, astern the hulk, there blazed half-way between the heaven and the sea, a mighty glow, and suddenly, as I stared, being dumb with admiration and surprise, I knew that it was the blaze of our fires upon the crown of the bigger hill; for, all the hill being in shadow, and hidden by the darkness, there showed only the glow of the fires, hung, as it were, in the void, and a very striking and beautiful spectacle it was. Then, as I watched, there came, abruptly a figure into view upon the edge of the glow, showing black and minute, and this I knew to be one of the men come to the edge of the hill to take a look at the hulk, or test the strain on the hawser. Now, upon my expressing admiration of the sight to Mistress Madison, she seemed greatly pleased, and told me that she had been up many times in the darkness to view it. And after that we went down again into the interior of the superstructure, and here the men were taking a further heave upon the big rope, before settling

the watches for the night, the which they managed, by
having one man at a time to keep awake and call the
rest whenever the hawser grew slack.

Later Mistress Madison showed me where I was to
sleep, and so, having bid one another a very warm
good-night, we parted, she going to see that her aunt
was comfortable, and I out on to the main-deck to
have a chat with the man on watch. In this way, I
passed the time until midnight, and in that while we
had been forced to call the men thrice to heave upon
the hawser, so quickly had the ship begun to make
way through the weed. Then, having grown sleepy, I
said good-night, and went to my berth, and so had
my first sleep upon a mattress, for some weeks.

Now when the morning was come, I waked, hearing
Mistress Madison calling upon me from the other side
of my door, and rating me very saucily for a lie-a-bed,
and at that I made good speed at dressing, and came
quickly into the saloon, where she had ready a breakfast that made me glad I had waked. But first, before
she would do aught else, she had me out to the look-
out place, running up before me most merrily and singing in the fullness of her glee, and so, when I had come
to the top of the superstructure, I perceived that she
had very good reason for so much merriment, and the
sight which came to my eyes, gladdened me most
mightily, yet at the same time filling me with a great
amazement; for, behold! in the course of that one night,
we had made near unto two hundred fathoms across
the weed, being now, with what we had made previously, no more than some thirty fathoms in from the
edge of the weed. And there stood Mistress Madison
beside me, doing somewhat of a dainty step-dance upon
the flooring of the look-out, and singing a quaint old
lilt that I had not heard that dozen years, and this little
thing, I think, brought back more clearly to me than
aught else how that this winsome maid had been lost
to the world for so many years, having been scarce of

the age of twelve when the ship had been lost in the weed-continent. Then, as I turned to make some remark, being filled with many feelings, there came a hail, from far above in the air, as it might be, and, looking up, I discovered the men upon the hill to be standing along the edge, and waving to us, and now I perceived how that the hill towered a very great way above us, seeming, as it were, to overhang the hulk though we were yet some seventy fathoms distant from the sheer sweep of its nearer precipe. And so, having waved back our greeting, we made down to breakfast, and, having come to the saloon, set-to upon the good victuals, and did very sound justice thereto.

Presently, having made an end of eating, and hearing the clack of the capstan-pawls, we hurried out on deck, and put our hands upon the bars, intending to join in that last heave which should bring the ship free out of her long captivity, and so for a time we moved round about the capstan, and I glanced at the girl beside me; for she had become very solemn, and indeed it was a strange and solemn time for her; for she, who had dreamed of the world as her childish eyes had seen it, was now, after many hopeless years, to go forth once more to it—to live in it, and to learn how much had been dreams, and how much real; and with all these thoughts I credited her; for they seemed such as would have come to me at such a time, and, presently, I made some blundering effort to show to her that I had understanding of the tumult which possessed her, and at that she smiled up at me with a sudden queer flash of sadness and merriment, and our glances met, and I saw something in hers, which was but newborn, and though I was but a young man, my heart interpreted it for me, and I was all hot suddenly with the pain and sweet delight of this new thing; for I had not dared to think upon that which already my heart had made bold to whisper to me, so that even thus soon I was miserable out of her presence. Then she looked downward at her hands upon the bar; and, in the same instant, there came a loud, abrupt cry from the second mate, to vast heaving, and at that all the men pulled out their bars and cast them upon the deck, and ran, shouting, to the ladder that led to the look-out, and we followed, and so came to the top, and discovered that at last the ship was clear of the weed, and floating in the open water between it and the island.

Now at the discovery that the hulk was free, the men commenced to cheer and shout in a very wild fashion, as, indeed, is no cause for wonder, and we cheered with them. Then, suddenly, in the midst of our shouting, Mistress Madison plucked me by the sleeve and pointed to the end of the island where the foot of the bigger hill jutted out in a great spur, and now I perceived a boat, coming round into view, and in another moment I saw that the bo'sun stood in the stern, steering; thus I knew that he must have finished repairing her whilst I had been on the hulk. By this, the men about us had discovered the nearness of the boat, and commenced shouting afresh, and they ran down, and to the bows of the vessel, and got ready a rope to cast. Now when the boat came near, the men in her scanned us very curiously; but the bo'sun took off his head-gear, with a clumsy grace that well became him; at which Mistress Madison smiled very kindly upon him, and, after that, she told me with great frankness that he pleased her, and, more, that she had never seen so great a man, which was not strange seeing that she had seen but few since she had come to years when men become of interest to a maid.

After saluting us the bo'sun called out to the second mate that he would tow us round to the far side of the island, and to this the officer agreed, being, I surmised, by no means sorry to put some solid matter between himself and the desolation of the great weed-continent; and so, having loosed the hawser, which fell from the hill-top with a prodigious splash, we had the boat ahead, towing. In this wise we opened out, presently, the end of the hill; but feeling now the force of the breeze, we bent a kedge to the hawser, and, the bo'sun carrying it seawards, we warped ourselves to windward of the island, and here, in forty fathoms, we vast heaving, and rode to the kedge.

Now when this was accomplished they called to our men to come aboard, and this they did, and spent all of that day in talk and eating; for those in the ship could scarce make enough of our fellows. And then, when it had come to night, they replaced that part of the superstructure which they had removed from about the head of the mizzen-stump, and so, all being secure, each one turned-in and had a full night's rest, of the which, indeed, many of them stood in sore need.

The following morning, the second mate had a consultation with the bo'sun, after which he gave the order to commence upon the removal of the great superstructure, and to this each one of us set himself with vigour. Yet it was a work requiring some time, and near five days had passed before we had the ship stripped clear. When this had been accomplished, there came a busy time of routing out various matter of which we should have need in jury rigging her; for they had been so long in disuse, that none remembered where to look for them. At this a day and half was spent, and after that we set-to about fitting her with such jury-masts as we could manage from our material.

Now, after the ship had been dismasted, all those seven years gone, the crew had been able to save many of her spars, these having remained attached to her, through their inability to cut away all of the gear; and though this had put them in sore peril at the time, of being sent to the bottom with a hole in their side, yet now had they every reason to be thankful; for, by this accident, we had now a foreyard, a topsail-yard, a

main t'gallant-yard, and the fore-topmast. They had
saved more than these; but had made use of the smaller
spars to shore up the superstructure, sawing them into
lengths for that purpose. Apart from such spars as they
had managed to secure, they had a spare topmast lashed
along under the larboard bulwarks, and a spare t'gallant
and royal-mast lying along the starboard side.

Now, the second mate and the bo'sun set the carpenter to work upon the spare topmast, bidding him
make for it some trestle-trees and bolsters, upon which
to lay the eyes of the rigging; but they did not trouble
him to shape it. Further, they ordered the same to be
fitted to the fore-topmast and the spare t'gallant and
royal-mast. And in the meanwhile, the rigging was prepared, and when this was finished, they made ready the
shears to hoist the spare topmast, intending this to take
the place of the main lower-mast. Then, when the carpenter had carried out their orders, he was set to make
three partners with a step cut in each, these being intended to take the heels of the three masts, and when
these were completed, they bolted them securely to the
decks at the fore part of each one of the stumps of
the three lower-masts. And so, having all ready, we
hove the main-mast into position, after which we proceeded to rig it. Now, when we had made an end of
this, we set-to upon the foremast, using for this the
fore-topmast which they had saved, and after that we
hove the mizzen-mast into place, having for this the
spare t'gallant and royal-mast.

Now the manner in which we secured the masts, before ever we came to the rigging of them, was by
lashing them to the stumps of the lower-masts, and
after we had lashed them, we drove dunnage and
wedges between the masts and the lashings, thus making
them very secure. And so, when we had set up the
rigging, we had confidence that they would stand all
such sail as we should be able to set upon them. Yet,
further than this, the bo'sun bade the carpenter make

wooden caps of six inch oak, these caps to fit over the *squared* heads of the lower-mast stumps, and having a hole, each of them, to embrace the jury-mast, and by making these caps in two halves, they were abled to bolt them on after the masts had been hove into position.

And so, having gotten in our three jury lower-masts, we hoisted up the foreyard to the main, to act as our mainyard, and did likewise with the topsail-yard to the fore, and after that, we sent up the t'gallant-yard to the mizzen. Thus we had her sparred, all but a bowsprit and jibboom; yet this we managed by making a stumpy, spike bowsprit from one of the smaller spars which had used to shore up the superstructure, and because we feared that it lacked strength to bear the strain of our fore and aft stays, we took down two hawsers from the fore, passing them in through the hawse-holes and setting them up there. And so we had her rigged, and, after that, we bent such sail as our gear abled us to carry, and in this wise had the hulk ready for sea.

Now, the time that it took us to rig the ship, and fit her out, was seven weeks, saving one day. And in all this time we suffered no molestation from any of the strange habitants of the weed-continent; though this may have been because we kept fires of dried weed going all the night about the decks, these fires being lit on big flat pieces of rock which we had gotten from the island. Yet, for all that we had not been troubled, we had more than once discovered strange things in the water swimming near to the vessel; but a flare of weed, hung over the side, on the end of a reed, had sufficed always to scare away such unholy visitants.

And so at last we came to the day on which we were in so good a condition that the bo'sun and the second mate considered the ship to be in a fit state to put to sea—the carpenter having gone over so much of her hull as he could get at and found her everywhere very sound; though her lower parts were hideously over-grown with weed, barnacles and other matters; yet this we could not help, and it was not wise to attempt to scrape her, having consideration to the creatures which we knew to abound in those waters.

Now in those seven weeks, Mistress Madison and I had come very close to one another, so that I had ceased to call her by any name save Mary, unless it were a dearer one than that; though this would be one of my own invention, and would leave my heart too naked did I put it down here.

Of our love one for the other, I think yet, and ponder how that mighty man, the bo'sun, came so quickly to a knowledge of the state of our hearts; for he gave me a very sly hint one day that he had a sound idea of the way in which the wind blew, and yet, though he said it with a half-jest, methought there was something wistful in his voice, as he spoke, and at that I just clapt my hand in his, and he gave it a very huge grip. And after that he ceased from the subject.

XVII: How We Came to Our Own Country

Now when the day came on which we made to leave the nearness of the island, and the waters of that strange sea, there was great lightness of heart among us, and we went very merrily about such tasks as were needful. And so, in a little, we had the kedge tripped, and had cast the ship's head to starboard, and presently, had her braced up upon the larboard tack, the which we managed very well; though our gear worked heavily, as might be expected. And after that we had gotten under way, we went to the lee side to witness the last of that lonesome island, and with us came the men of the ship, and so, for a space, there was a silence among us; for they were very quiet, looking astern and saying naught; but we had sympathy with them, knowing somewhat of those past years.

And now the bo'sun came to the break of the poop, and called down to the men to muster aft, the which they did, and I with them; for I had come to regard them as my very good comrades; and rum was served out to each of them, and to me along with the rest, and it was Mistress Madison herself who dipped it out to us from the wooden bucket; though it was the buxom woman who had brought it up from the lazarette. Now, after the rum, the bo'sun bade the crew to clear up the

gear about the decks, and get matters secured, and at
that I turned to go with the men, having become so
used to work with them; but he called to me to come up
to him upon the poop, the which I did, and there he
spoke respectfully, remonstrating with me, and remind-
ing me that now there was need no longer for me to
toil; for that I was come back to my old position of
passenger, such as I had been in the *Glen Carrig,* ere
she foundered. But to this talk of his, I made reply that
I had as good a right to work my passage home as any
other among us; for though I had paid for a passage in
the *Glen Carrig,* I had done no such thing regarding
the *Seabird*—this being the name of the hulk—; and to
this, my reply, the bo'sun said little; but I perceived
that he liked my spirit, and so from thence until we
reached the Port of London, I took my turn and part
in all seafaring matters, having become by this quite
proficient in the calling. Yet, in one matter, I availed
myself of my former position; for I chose to live aft,
and by this was abled to see much of my sweetheart,
Mistress Madison.

Now after dinner upon the day on which we left the
island, the bo'sun and the second mate picked the
watches, and thus I found myself chosen to be in the
bo'sun's, at which I was mightily pleased. And when
the watches had been picked, they had all hands to
'bout ship, the which, to the pleasure of all, she accomplished; for under such gear and with so much growth
upon her bottom, they had feared that we should have
to veer, and by this we should have lost much distance
to leeward, whereas we desired to edge so much to windward as we could, being anxious to put space between
us and the weed-continent. And twice more that day we
put the ship about, though the second time it was to
avoid a great bank of weed that lay floating athwart
our bows; for all the sea to windward of the island,
so far as we had been able to see from the top of the
higher hill, was studded with floating masses of the

weed, like unto thousands of islets, and in places like to far-spreading reefs. And, because of these, the sea all about the island remained very quiet and unbroken, so that there was never any surf, no, nor scarce a broken wave upon its shore, and this, for all that the wind had been fresh for many days.

When the evening came, we were again upon the larboard tack, making, perhaps, some four knots in the hour; though, had we been in proper rig, and with a clean bottom, we had been making eight or nine, with so good a breeze and so calm a sea. Yet, so far, our progress had been very reasonable; for the island lay, maybe, some five miles to leeward, and about fifteen astern. And so we prepared for the night. Yet, a little before dark, we discovered that the weed-continent trended out towards us; so that we should pass it, maybe, at a distance of something like half a mile, and, at that, there was talk between the second mate and the bo'sun as to whether it was better to put the ship about, and gain a greater sea-room before attempting to pass this promontory of weed; but at last they decided that we had naught to fear; for we had fair way through the water, and further, it did not seem reasonable to suppose that we should have aught to fear from the habitants of the weed-continent, at so great a distance as the half of a mile. And so we stood on; for, once past the point, there was much likelihood of the weed trending away to the Eastward, and if this were so, we could square-in immediately and get the wind upon our quarter, and so make better way.

Now it was the bo'sun's watch from eight of the evening until midnight, and I, with another man, had the look-out until four bells. Thus it chanced that, coming abreast of the point during our time of watching, we peered very earnestly to leeward; for the night was dark, having no moon until nearer the morning; and we were full of unease in that we had come so near again to the desolation of that strange continent. And then, suddenly, the man with me clutched my shoulder, and pointed into the darkness upon our bow, and thus I discovered that we had come nearer to the weed than the bo'sun and the second mate had intended; they, without doubt, having miscalculated our leeway. At this, I turned and sang out to the bo'sun that we were near to running upon the weed, and, in the same moment, he shouted to the helmsman to luff, and directly afterwards our starboard side was brushing against the great outlying tufts of the point, and so, for a breathless minute, we waited. Yet the ship drew clear, and so into the open water beyond the point; but I had seen something as we scraped against the weed, a sudden glimpse of white, gliding among the growth, and then I saw others, and, in a moment, I was down on the main-deck, and running aft to the bo'sun; yet midway along the deck a horrid shape came above the starboard rail, and I gave out a loud cry of warning. Then I had a capstan-bar from the rack near, and smote with it at the thing, crying all the while for help, and at my blow the thing went from my sight, and the bo'sun was with me, and some of the men.

Now the bo'sun had seen my stroke, and so sprang upon the t'gallant rail, and peered over; but gave back on the instant, shouting to me to run and call the other watch, for that the sea was full of the monsters swimming off to the ship, and at that I was away at a run, and when I had waked the men, I raced aft to the cabin and did likewise with the second mate, and so returned in a minute, bearing the bo'sun's cutlass, my own cut-and-thrust, and the lantern that hung always in the saloon. Now when I had gotten back, I found all things in a mighty scurry—men running about in their shirts and drawers, some in the galley bringing fire from the stove, and others lighting a fire of dry weed to lee-ward of the galley, and along the starboard rail there was already a fierce fight, the men using capstan-bars, even as I had done. Then I thrust the bo'sun's cutlass into his hand, and at that he gave a great shout, part of joy, and part of approbation, and after that he snatched the lantern from me, and had run to the larboard side of the deck, before I was well aware that he had taken the light; but now I followed him, and happy it was for all of us in the ship that he had thought to go at that moment; for the light of the lantern showed me the vile faces of three of the weed men climbing over the larboard rail; yet the bo'sun had cleft them or ever I could come near; but in a moment I was full busy; for there came nigh a dozen heads above the rail a little aft of where I was, and at that I ran at them, and did good execution; but some had been aboard, if the bo'sun had not come to my help. And now the decks were full of light, several fires having been lit, and the second mate having brought out fresh lanterns; and now the men had gotten their cutlasses, the which were more handy than the capstan-bars; and so the fight went forward, some having come over to our side to help us, and a very wild sight it must have seemed to any onlooker; for all about the decks burned the fires and the lanterns, and along the rails ran the men, smiting at hideous faces that rose in dozens into the wild glare of our fighting lights. And everywhere drifted the stench of the brutes. And up on the poop, the fight was as brisk as elsewhere; and here, having been drawn by a cry for help, I discovered the buxom woman smiting with a gory meat-axe at a vile thing which had gotten a clump of its tentacles upon her dress; but she had dispatched it, or ever my sword could help her, and then, to my astonishment, even at that time of peril, I discovered the captain's wife, wielding a small sword, and the face of her was like to the face of a tiger; for her mouth was drawn, and showed her teeth clenched; but she uttered no word nor cry, and I doubt not but that she had some vague idea that she worked her husband's vengeance.

Then, for a space, I was as busy as any, and after-

wards I ran to the buxom woman to demand the whereabouts of Mistress Madison, and she, in a very breathless voice, informed me that she had locked her in her
room out of harm's way, and at that I could have em-
braced the woman; for I had been sorely anxious to
know that my sweetheart was safe.

And, presently, the fight diminished, and so, at last,
came to an end, the ship having drawn well away from
the point, and being now in the open. And after that
I ran down to my sweetheart, and opened her door,
and thus, for a space, she wept, having her arms about
my neck; for she had been in sore terror for me, and
for all the ship's company. But, soon, drying her tears,
she grew very indignant with her nurse for having
locked her into her room, and refused to speak to that
good woman for near an hour. Yet I pointed out to
her that she could be of very great use in dressing such
wounds as had been received, and so she came back to
her usual brightness, and brought out bandages, and
lint, and ointment, and thread, and was presently very
busy.

Now it was later that there rose a fresh commotion
in the ship; for it had been discovered that the captain's
wife was a-missing. At this, the bo'sun and the second
mate instituted a search; but she was nowhere to be
found, and, indeed, none in the ship ever saw her again,
at which it was presumed that she had been dragged
over by some of the weed men, and so come upon her
death. And at this, there came a great prostration to
my sweetheart so that she would not be comforted for
the space of nigh three days, by which time the ship
had come clear of those strange seas, having left the
incredible desolation of the weed-continent far under
our starboard counter.

And so, after a voyage which lasted for nine and
seventy days since getting under weigh, we came to the
Port of London, having refused all offers of assistance
on the way.

Now here, I had to say farewell to my comrades of so many months and perilous adventures; yet, being a man not entirely without means, I took care that each of them should have a certain gift by which to remember me.

And I placed monies in the hands of the buxom woman, so that she could have no reason to stint my sweetheart, and she having—for the comfort of her conscience—taken her good man to the church, set up a little house upon the borders of my estate; but this was not until Mistress Madison had come to take her place at the head of my hall in the County of Essex.

Now one further thing there is of which I must tell. Should any, chancing to trespass upon my estate, come upon a man of very mighty proportions, albeit somewhat bent by age, seated comfortably at the door of his little cottage, then shall they know him for my friend the bo'sun; for to this day do he and I foregather, and let our talk drift to the desolate places of this earth, pondering upon that which we have seen—the weed-continent, where reigns desolation and the terror of its strange habitants. And, after that, we talk softly of the land where God hath made monsters after the fashion of trees. Then, maybe, my children come about me, and so we change to other matters; for the little ones love not terror.

THE REIGN OF WIZARDRY

JACK WILLIAMSON

THE GREATEST MAGICAL ISLAND THE WORLD HAD EVER KNOWN

Crete — the dread island of wizardry where the power of Minos was guarded by three walls. The land where every nine years the Minoan games decided the fate of Crete's famed ruler. Where the winner stood to gain the hand of Ariadne, the treasure of Knossos — and command of the formidable Dark One's powers. So it was that the pirate, Theseus, came to the Minoan empire, determined to conquer and destroy. Alone he faced Minos and Daedalus in a struggle against totally overwhelming odds . . .

FANTASY   0 7221 9185 5   £1.50

And don't miss Jack Williamson's classic *Legion of Space* trilogy:

THE LEGION OF SPACE
ONE AGAINST THE LEGION
THE COMETEERS

— Also available in Sphere Books.

A SELECTION OF TITLES FROM SPHERE

FICTION

STILL MISSING	Beth Gutcheon	£1.75 ☐
INHERITORS OF THE STORM	Victor Sondheim	£4.95 ☐
NIGHT PROBE!	Clive Cussler	£1.95 ☐
CHIMERA	Stephen Gallagher	£1.75 ☐
PALOMINO	Danielle Steel	£1.75 ☐

FILM & TV TIE-INS

ON THE LINE	Anthony Minghella	£1.25 ☐
FAME	Leonore Fleischer	£1.50 ☐
FIREFOX	Craig Thomas	£1.75 ☐
GREASE II	William Rotsler	£1.25 ☐
CONAN THE BARBARIAN	L. Sprague de Camp & Lin Carter	£1.25 ☐

NON-FICTION

BEFORE I FORGET	James Mason	£2.25 ☐
TOM PILGRIM: AUTOBIOGRAPHY OF A SPIRITUALIST HEALER	Tom Pilgrim	£1.50 ☐
YOUR CHILD AND THE ZODIAC	Teri King	£1.50 ☐
THE SURVIVOR	Jack Eisner	£1.75 ☐

All Sphere books are available at your local bookshop or newsagent, or can be ordered direct from the publisher. Just tick the titles you want and fill in the form below.

Name _____

Address _____

_____

Write to Sphere Books, Cash Sales Department, P.O. Box 11, Falmouth, Cornwall TR10 9EN

Please enclose a cheque or postal order to the value of the cover price plus:

UK: 45p for the first book, 20p for the second book and 14p for each additional book ordered to a maximum charge of £1.63.

OVERSEAS: 75p for the first book plus 21p per copy for each additional book.

BFPO & EIRE: 45p for the first book, 20p for the second book plus 14p per copy for the next 7 books, thereafter 8p per book.

Sphere Books reserve the right to show new retail prices on covers which may differ from those previously advertised in the text or elsewhere, and to increase postal rates in accordance with the PO.